# THE JOURNEY

One Person's Vacation of
a Lifetime is a Migrants
Journey to a New World

J.A.Tucker

What causes someone to leave the comfort of their home and their country of birth? Why do people make life changing decisions to uproot and travel across continents in search of the "promised land"?

Could you leave your home, travel across vast countries and move somewhere with only the shirt on your back and the contents of your home in your pockets?

From famine, civil war or lack of prospects to even just hope of a better life, thousands of people every year are forced to move home.

Journey is a story of hope and the sheer desire to live in peace and safety. Can it make you question your own beliefs and ponder the question of immigration and our values as citizens on the planet we share with billions of other lives.

Why is it that our immediate thought of immigration is negativity? Is it something which has been handled so poorly by our governments for so long that we've forgotten the true reasons why the masses are turning to our own shores for help?

Perhaps we need to rethink?...

# The Journey

By J.A Tucker

# CHAPTER 1

Sitting, huddled in the corner of the boat, the small boy was looking down at the floor. The thought of looking up once again terrified him. The sight of his parents looking worried for their lives ran cold and sharply through the boy's body. Until this point, he'd never seen the look of terror on his father's face. Though troubled, his father mostly kept his thoughts to himself and managed to put a brave face on even at the most difficult of times. However the situation at hand was enough for even his father to crack. The vision of panic on his father's face was one which left him feeling more scared than ever before in his life.

The sea was only now starting to darken. Moments before had the child looked up and seen the sun dipping beneath the dark clouds on the horizon. Up until now, the sun had been a source of light and warmth. But now, with the onset of darkness and the storm clouds rapidly approaching, the situation was quickly turning from calm to panic and was noticeable on the faces of many passengers.

As the tip of the sun licked the edge of the horizon, it was only a matter of minutes before darkness was upon them. A small light was hanging next to the man piloting the boat. However with the large number of people all crowded together, the dim light didn't carry much further than quarter of the way towards the back.

As the sun finally set, the sea was now completely black with no light hitting it whatsoever. The approaching storm clouds were rolling over the boat and small droplets of rain were falling all around them.

Light droplets of rain quietly tapping on the sea quickly turned to heavy and from being minutes away, the storm was well and truly over them. During the day, the sea had never been calm, however now started to increase in height, making the dimly lit horizon impossible to see. The once manageable voyage was quickly becoming a treacherous one.

The wind had started to whistle around the people and the small boy, still looking down at the floor, felt the cold wind wrap around his body as he hugged himself tighter to fight the noise of the storm.

One wave after another hit the boat and from being dry, the floor was now drenched and small puddles were quickly forming around the people. Another wave crashed against the side of the boat and a huge gush of water fell over the people, soaking every person in its path.

To this point, the voyage had been difficult, but no one had expected this kind of weather. The summer was well and truly upon them and poor weather was something they simply didn't expect. At no point during the day had it looked a possibility there might be even a drop of rain.

The young boy, though tucked down low in the corner of the boat, was now, like many of the other passengers, being tossed from side to side. His father grabbed him with a hand to try and keep themselves together. He could hear his mother crying and wailing as she was being tormented by the waves and the rocking of the boat. He saw as his father also grabbed his mother and the three of them were huddled in the corner together, trying to shelter themselves against the stormy conditions. But it was no use. The waves were leaping over their heads and the wind now catapulted small droplets of water onto their faces and hands, stinging as each droplet hit them. Escaping the deluge of water was impossible.

Amongst the shouting and screaming a voice could be heard, yelling at the pilot to speed the boat up. Wherever they were heading in the dark, it was obvious they had now focused their attentions on getting there faster. Escaping this storm was now top priority and they sped the boat up.

'Father!' yelled the boy as the boat was hit harder than ever before by the onslaught and sheer power of the sea crashing into it. It felt like minutes as the boat jumped into the air, crashing back down into the water, making the most terrifying of noises as it landed so violently.

'Don't worry child, I won't let you go' His father shouted at the boy, trying to make his voice heard over the wind, rain and screams from other passengers.

The storm had now turned even more violent. The small boy screamed as the thunder rattled his body. It felt like even his teeth rattled inside of his mouth. Another bolt of lightning came and was quickly followed by yet another clap of thunder, again, crashing around each and every passenger. There was no escaping the deluge of water, wind and deafening sound of thunder.

The boy took a moment and plucked up the courage to look up. Wiping the water from his eyes, he could see the boat being rocked from side to side. The dim light at the front of the boat was enough to light up the rain as it rushed downwards towards the people. Very few passengers were standing, most were lying, crouching or sitting on the floor. However the boy could see out of the corner of his eye, one man attempt to stand up and stagger slowly, edging his way to the front of the boat towards the pilot. The man standing next to him, held out a gun and pointed it towards him. The boy could hardly see what was happening, nor could he hear the men shouting at one another. He could just about make out the man with the gun motion for the other man to sit down. Holding out his hands, the man begged and pleaded for help to do something about the situation.

Another wave crashed heavily against the boat and the dim light was tossed from side to side, lighting up one side of the boat to the other. Much like before, the boat jumped out of the water and landed heavily as it hit the sea. The light swung back towards where the pleading man was once standing. The boy just about caught sight of the man's feet falling out of the boat and into the sea. People around him were screaming as a few people looked over the boat and tried with all their might to grab hold of the man before he was pulled away. However it was no use, the boat had already moved meters away and continued on its route. Looking behind the boat there was nothing, no colour, no sky, no water, no man. Whoever he was who'd fallen from the boat, he was now gone, lost to the sea. The boat continued on its journey.

The man with the gun raised it once more and pointed it towards the people from where the man had originally stood. The boy could just about hear as he yelled at the people to stay calm and stay down.

Minutes passed as the boat continued on its path. Cutting through the waves at a rate of knots and being bashed from side to side as yet more waves barraged the sides with enough force to bend steal.

The boy again looked down at his feet, feeling petrified to look up again, even his father and mother were facing down and were now praying to God, begging for forgiveness and for safe passage.

Crash after crash came, as the deluge of water fell upon them. The small boy felt his father's grip loosen as he struggled to hold onto his family in the turbulent and soaking conditions.

Another loud bang came from close to where they were sitting, however this time the noise felt mechanical, like something had struck the side of the boat. The screams and yelling, which had started to die down had now returned. The man with the gun grabbed the light next to him and shone it towards where the noise had come from. As he did so, the small boy could see a gaping hole in the side of the boat and could see water rushing both inwards and outwards. The boat again jumping as a huge wave catapulted it into the air. His father's grip failed him for the last time.

Through the dim light and pouring rain, the small boy saw as his mother was sucked into the void of the hole. The father's grip had failed him at the wrong time and his mother could do nothing as the boat was tossed upwards by the sea and she slid helplessly towards the gaping hole. Person after person were dragged away from their loved ones who could do nothing but hold out hands, whilst still trying to grab hold of the boat for their own safety.

The last thing the boy saw from his corner of the boat, was his mothers hands desperately trying to grab part of the side before the sea clutched at her torso and pulled her into the blackness around them.


Panting for breath, Jude sprung upwards from his mattress, attempting to make sense of his surroundings. The reality of being awake quickly came over him and he realised he'd had another nightmare and this time it was more vivid than the last. This would be yet another nightmare which would haunt him for the remainder of the night. But despite the haunting thoughts of his bad dream, he eventually fell back to sleep.

# CHAPTER 2

'Hurry up Belle, we're all waiting for you!' Shouted Vicky from the bottom of the stairs. 'Jude's already in the car, come on!' Shouting once more up the stairs towards her slow moving teenage daughter.

As Belle came down the stairs, she casually walked past her mother, not giving her a second look as she walked straight out of the house and into the passenger seat of the family car.

'I'll shut the door then Belle!' Vicky sarcastically said whilst slamming the front door behind her and walking to the driver's side. 'Honestly, must we always go through the same rigmarole when we leave the house?'

'Oh for goodness sake mum, must we always have the same conversation every time we go out, I mean why do I even have to come anyway?' Belle asked.

'Because dear, it was your idea that we go on

a cruise this year and being that your father is at work, I'd like some input on exactly where it is we go. Plus...' Taking a brief pause and sighing before she continued. 'You're part of this family and I want you to be engaged with the family this holiday. Belle you'll be going off to university soon and this is more than likely going to be your last family holiday. That's why I didn't mind you choosing the destination, because I want us all to have one last holiday together, one which we'll always remember. You're still my little girl Belle, I kind of want things to be like they were... before you became all hormonal and only interested in boys and school'

'Yeah yeah, okay mum I get it.'

Belle looked up from her phone, she placed it in her jacket pocket and gave her mum a rare and deeply appreciated smile.

Belle's relationship with her father was close, and always had been. However in recent years her relationship with her mother was strained. Since Belle had become a teenager, she'd almost lost touch with her mother, much like any mother/teenage daughter relationship. Vicky clung onto the hope that when she eventually left for university and became homesick, their relationship may again be strong. But for now, she would take whatever crumbs were thrown her way. Today's crumbs were in the form of a rare smile and the fact she'd placed her phone down for a short while and was going into town with them. "Little Vicky victories" she told herself every time Belle gave her some form of love or affection.

'Seeing as we're on our way to town mum, I don't suppose we could pop into the phone shop? I really need a new phone, this battery just doesn't hold charge for any longer than five hours'

'And you know why that is Belle, it's because you're on your phone non-stop. Maybe if you put it down for a while, it might hold its charge for longer'

Belle's father, Michael, had given her his old phone a year back. Although it was a year older than her friends models, it still did the job of keeping her up to date with her friends status and kept her amused. The phone's battery issues weren't all that bad and for the time being didn't justify the purchase of an upgrade.

Belle had been constantly haggling with her mother and father for a new phone and it was clear that it was a case of having a newer, more higher spec model than a technical problem as she was claiming.

'Look, we can't afford a new one at the moment. I know you desperately would like one, but now simply isn't the time. Perhaps closer to Christmas, maybe a joint Christmas and birthday present together'

Belle sighed, however she knew that money was a little tight in the house and despite her typical teenage attitude, she knew when to push and when not to push her parents. This was one of those instances where she realised that pushing wasn't the right thing to do. Plus waiting another few months may not be the worst thing in the world. She agreed with her mother and said thanks with a warm smile on her face.

Vicky wanted to offer her children everything they wanted, but at the same time wanted them to appreciate things, and for the best part, they both did. Belle had a part time job and because of studying, her mother only let her work once at the weekend. This only gave Belle enough money for the week ahead and not to spend on lavish items, like a new phone. For the time being, she would still be financially reliant on her parents. This was something her mother and father were comfortable with. Once again, the small offering of a smile thrown towards her mother had given Vicky her second "Vicky victory" of the day.

Walking down the high street, the three of them looked onwards towards the travel agency. Vicky had used the same agency since she was the same age as her daughter, booking a girl's holiday to Spain when she herself was eighteen. Although the staff had changed, it was still run by the same management and had the family's details on file. Because of their loyalty, in coming back year on year out, they always received a small discount.

Vicky opened the door and allowed both Belle and Jude in first. An agent looked up and asked if she could help. They walked over and took a seat.

'So how can I help the three of you today?'

'We're after a cruise for the family, it's kind of a last minute thing, something in the coming month. We've not done a cruise before, only resorts and hotels. However this is probably my daughters last holiday with us and we gave her the option of where to go and what to do.' Vicky glanced over at Belle, who was remarkably paying attention and not on her phone.

'Okay so it's for the three of you or...' The agent asked not wanting to assume there was a father on the scene.

'No, there's four of us, my husband's working, so it's entirely up to us where we go.'

The agent looked at Jude. 'And where would you like to go young man?' She asked whilst smiling at him.

Jude looked shocked by the question. He was seven and despite being fairly clever, he wasn't the most switched on of children. When they'd first mentioned about going on a cruise, he assumed it would be a small speed boat. He never really got the idea of what a cruise was until Vicky had shown him a picture of a cruise liner on the internet and told him they'd be living on a boat for two weeks.

Although a little apprehensive at first, Jude had started to show some signs of coming round to the idea. Jude's fear of the water had been there throughout his life. Despite having regular swimming lessons, water was still something he was scared of, though more open water these days. Vicky and Michael both hoped that being on a cruise for two weeks would help his fear and he'd start to get used to the idea of the sea not being something to be feared of.

'Jude's a little quiet today I'm afraid, he had a rough night's sleep and woke up all tired. But we were thinking of doing a Mediterranean cruise?' She explained to the travel agent whilst looking at Jude.

John was having "one of those days". Nothing was really going to plan and he'd spent most of the day standing in the high street under an umbrella. But at least now the rain and dark clouds had passed from overhead there were a few more people walking about.

Most of John's life had been a bit of a train wreck; a broken home, lack of education and little work as an adult. However a few months ago, he was offered a place at a local charity and it had been a real turnaround for him. The money wasn't particularly good and in a few instances he'd been spoken down to or even completely ignored. But the one good thing this job had was the staff. His whole life he'd spent trying to get attention from people. After splitting from John's mother, his father had decided he didn't have time for a son. After a few years of persistent attempts to have a relationship with him, John had decided that no contact was better than irregular, once sometimes twice a year. He had a relationship with his mother, however even she wanted to spend most of her free time with various boyfriends rather than her own son. As soon as John was old enough, he moved out and in with friends. His friends had been the only positive contact he'd had with people and even they moved on after having families of their own. Up until this job, John had felt alone and in limbo, unsure of where his life was heading or to which path he should take.

The people John worked with all had something in common and most seemed to need something more in their lives. There was the grandmother who wanted to get back into working life after retirement had gone stale. The work experience staff who wanted something different to put on their CV or the people who simply wanted to give something back to society and chose a charity. There were no exceptions, everyone wanted something positive from this work and for John that was no different. The moral was good, working closely with people from all walks of life was an experience of its own and the regular work was proving to be something useful to focus his mind on.

Every person who he walked up to, he held his head up high, he never sighed, never cussed or even battered an eyelid when someone told him to "sod off and get a proper job". He enjoyed the experience and had decided a long time ago to use it for good in his life.


'Come on you lot' Cried Vicky as she dragged the children out of the travel agency. Her husband Michael had finished work early and was hanging around in town waiting for his family to join him. He was excited at the prospect of a different sort of holiday and was equally happy that Vicky had managed to drag Belle out of the house and into town with them. They rarely spent time together these days, so to have his entire family with him would be a treat, maybe they'd all go out for dinner together.

'Do you think Dad will like what we've booked?' Belle asked her mother as they walked speedily down the high street.

'Yes, he's really looking forward to spending time with all of us and especially as this potentially will be the last time we all go away together. He just wants us all to have a nice time away. I don't think he's even that bothered by where we go, though I do know he didn't want a long transit, so a Mediterranean cruise is perfect for that. Thanks for your help today Belle, it was nice to have your input.'

They hurried down the street, bristly walking passed the various shops, blanking the beggar outside the bank selling magazines and almost knocking over the charity worker desperately trying to get their attention.

'Mum you almost knocked that guy over!' Belle told her mother whilst looking back at the man picking up his clipboard from the floor.

'Oh he should get a proper job rather than standing there in the middle of the high street in every ones way' she said whilst still racing towards her husband's office.

'Michael!' Vicky shouted as they all quickly approached him.

'Have you booked something fun for us?' He asked as they greeted him.

'Yes, Dad' Jude said whilst giving his father a high-five. 'We're going on a cruise to Greece!'.

As John picked up his dripping wet clipboard off the floor, he caught a glimpse of the young girl looking back at him with sorrow on her face. A colleague walked over to him and patted him on the shoulder. 'That was rude!' She said whilst picking up John's pen from the floor.

As John brushed the dirt off his clipboard, he took a deep breath, held his head high and placed a smile back on his face. He wouldn't let the bad attitude of the few ruin his day.

# CHAPTER 3

Every step had become arduous, much like the feeling you get when you've been walking for a long time without rest. The dry conditions made for a dusty and dirty path ahead and the dragging of feet made for more flickering of dust and small stones getting trapped inside the shoes of many of the people. For most, it was just something they dealt with, however for the young boy travelling towards the back of the group of walker's, it was really starting to be an annoyance. Doing this long of a walk was certainly not something he was used to nor particularly wanted to do. He never really understood why they were walking so far and never got a straight answer from his parents. It almost felt like they were hiding something from him. However he was only a young boy of seven and regardless of what his father would have said to him, it would have been fairly incomprehensible for the young boy. They'd been away from home for a few weeks now and he was missing home. He missed the mountains, the huge towering rocks which always seemed to cast a shadow in front of him. They were always in his life, he'd never travelled anywhere without them being around him and now they'd been replaced by the rough, dusty flat terrain, he longed for them once more. He missed his friends and he missed the goats.

The distance covered, even over a short period, had been less than before and for all the people within the party, each day had been more difficult than the previous. Finally, before twilight, they'd all come to a decision they needed to take a rest and set up camp.

His sister had been holding him by the hand for the majority of the afternoon, whilst his mother and father had been walking behind, talking to a few of the other people from within the party.

'Sit down and rest' his sister told him as he stood watching his parents from a far. He was unsure what they were doing, however it was clear that today's walk was over. Even at the age of seven and being full of energy, he'd now started to find the constant walking a strain on his legs and feet and was beginning to wonder if his parent's choice of travel was the smartest.

Sitting down on the dusty floor, he looked aimlessly at his parents as they moved towards him. He loved them both dearly, however had a special father son relationship. His father always put his son first and they shared a special bond. Notably it was the smaller things that spoke a thousand words. The smiles, hugs, even the offering of food from his own plate and always the offer of a drink from his father's cup when he was thirsty. There was nothing he wanted more in his life than the love from his parents and it was clear they both loved him and his sister unconditionally.

As his father walked over, he stood up to face him. 'Father?' he asked as he was patted on the shoulder and told him to again sit down. His father continued to walk past him and over to the man in front of them. After a few minutes he walked back over to his son and daughter, who was also sitting on the dusty floor.

'How much longer father?' he asked as his father stood in front of him looking him in the eye.

'Not much longer my son, we're camping here over-night and will stay here for a few days. It's a good location near the river my son. Go and fetch my bow and arrow and we'll try and find some dinner' he said whilst smiling at the boy.

He loved hunting with his father. They always did it alone, just the two of them and it reminded him of home. It was a good feeling that he got from spending time like this with his father and he was often handed the bow to practice with. On this particular trip, he'd been given more opportunity than before to practice. He was still not old enough to kill an animal yet and certainly wasn't practiced enough to respectfully kill. His father had always told him that killing one of God's creations was not something that should be taken lightly. It was a privilege to hunt and be permitted to kill an animal for its flesh. His father always made the point of only firing an arrow when it had the ability to kill instantly. 'My son, if you miss and only injure the animal, it will bleed and feel pain. That pain is felt everywhere, the trail of blood on the ground will tell a story to God's creatures elsewhere of the pain felt by the dying animal. You always kill wisely and with respect and lastly my son, you thank the creature for giving its life to you.'

It was a story he always told his son whenever they went on a hunting trip and on this particular day, despite the fact his father looked exhausted, it was no exception.

The boy handed his father his bow and arrow and they walked off towards the small river and down the bank towards the rocks. They were looking for tracks of any animals which may have passed through recently, then use those tracks to attempt to find the animal.

His father was a good hunter and very rarely did he come home empty handed. There was always something in his hands, whether rabbit, fish or even a rat. On this day they'd caught sign of a rabbit, perhaps a few. There were fresh droppings on the ground as well as a few signs of tracks in the dust. They both knelt down and studied the tracks. The small scuff marks on the ground were giving the rabbits last movements away and it was clear to the experienced hunter which way the animal was moving.

'Look at these tracks my son, you can see they're deep at the front, in the direction to which the rabbit was heading. They each tail off at the back. There, can you see where it has turned?' The scuffs on the ground swiped right, then again headed straight towards a bush. There was a small hole in the bush, a route used by many animal, heading directly through it. There was a small tuft of fur left on some of the twigs and bush.

They both crouched down, the bow hanging over the shoulder of the father who had his arm over his sons shoulder. The father pointed towards the hole.

'There boy, look! You see the old fur here, it's lighter in colour and is thinner. This animal travels through this bush regularly. Let us continue and see if we can find its burrow. If not, we'll set a trap for it here and wait.'

Twilight was well and truly upon them and the sky was full of red and blue. It was a beautiful evening and other than the trickle of water lapping on the side of the small river, it was very quiet. They'd walked far enough away from the party of people to not hear them. Although they were out of ear shot of the camp site, they could see a fire raging in the background, five to six hundred yards away and it would act as their beacon when they decided to head back.

'Shush!' The man said to his son 'don't move.' He could hear something in front of them, no more than fifty feet away. There was a faint noise, though it sounded louder than what they were hunting and for a second it took the child's father by surprise. He pulled his bow from his shoulder and lined an arrow towards where the noise was coming from.

'What is it father?' Whispered the child as he remained low.

'I don't know, but I'm certain it's not the rabbit. Stay close to my side and stay vigilant.'

The light was fading and the shadows on the floor had all but faded as the sun had finally vanished beneath the horizon. It was becoming harder to see and the once easy rabbit tracks to trace had become all but forgotten in the darkness.

They both continued to slowly creep forward, remaining low and treading carefully so as not to make any sudden noises. Whatever it was out there, it was something large enough to concern the boy's father and grab the attention of the forward facing arrow. They continued slowly, arrow pointing directly in front of them. Again, another noise came from in front of them and they paused. Assessing the situation, the father decided to continue. Whatever it was ahead of them, would need to be found. It was either food and enough to feed them for a few days or something harsher that might pose a threat to them in the night. The fire around the campsite would be one thing, but to completely eliminate a threat would be more the wiser option.

The child looked up to his father and could see there was no worry nor concern in his face, only the careful, considerate and well practised face of a hunter. He felt completely at ease by his father's side and was worried about nothing. It was sheer excitement the boy was feeling and the exhilaration of hunting something large with his father was overwhelming.

Something was ahead of them, the other side of a large bush. Because of the dimming light and the thickness of the bush, they would have to slowly walk around it and catch whatever it was by surprise.

'Stay here my son, I have this.'

'No father, I want to come, you might need me.'

He handed his son a knife which was hanging from his side. 'Take it boy and only use it if I tell you to.' The boy had never held his father's hunting knife before. It was heavier than he imagined and the moonlight glistened off the sharp blade. He felt proud to hold it, to be trusted with its power.

The child held the knife aloft and both father and son continued around the bush. Still crouching and moving slowly, they crept, the father in front with the son just behind his shoulder. The noise came again, this time a little louder and it was clear this was a large animal, something that would take a precise arrow to take down quickly. As they neared the corner, they could see something, it wasn't clear what it was, however it hadn't heard them and was still, looking the other way.

'Father, take this.' The boy handed his father a small rock. The father knew what to do with it, the two of them had used the trick many times in the past together. They'd often throw the rock away from the animal and startle it from the opposite side of them. Then whilst the animal was startled they would ambush it as it ran into their direction. The father making the kill even before the animal had time to react.

'Are you ready my son?' 'Yes father.' He passed the rock back to the child and told him where to throw it. Taking firm grasp of the weapon he decisively pointed it toward the faint shadow of the animal.

The boy raised his hand and threw the rock away from them. They heard the animal turn and speedily father and son rounded the corner, both arrow and knife pointing towards the animal, poised for attack.

Fighting against every one of his instincts to fire, the father halted quickly in his tracks. It was no animal.

# CHAPTER 4

Vicky sat on a bench at the front of the balcony, overlooking the swimming lanes. It was the same uncomfortable bench which her parents had sat at years ago when she herself was learning to swim and attended diving lessons. The warmth from the swimming pool and chlorine in the air was comforting. Despite her decision to stop diving classes all those years back, she still found comfort from the pool. Now Vicky sat up on the balcony, watching as ten children stood side by side at the edge of the water awaiting instruction from the teacher to jump in.

Taking another sip of tea from her cup, Vicky placed it back down to her side, took another bite of her bar of chocolate and rested it on a napkin next to the tea.

One by one the children jumped into the water. Jude was the last child along the line and as the children prior to him jumped, Vicky felt like she could telepathically sense how Jude was feeling. He didn't particularly like the water, however both his parents had pushed him into swimming lessons. They both persevered in their fight for him to continue the lessons, even after his armbands had been taken away. But regardless of his continued lessons and the occasional enjoyment he took from the water, he still suffered with a deep resolute fear that simply wouldn't diminish.

For both Vicky and Michael, they were more content with the fact that Jude could now swim. If he ever got into trouble in the water, at least he'd be able to swim or at least stay afloat whilst someone pulled him out.

The echo of the children jumping and splashing into the pool rang around Jude's ears and he felt extremely uneasy at the thought of being pressured into jumping. The loudness of his swimming teachers voice and echo from her whistle, the splash as the children jumped and the thought of being next… Jude jumped without noticeable hesitation. He closed his eyes and held his nose as he jumped and in the moment before his feet touched the water, he felt an even greater sense of dread. As he hit the water, within a micro second it closed in around him and swallowed him, cocooning him until the moment he raised his head for air.

Vicky watched as her son was momentarily taken by the pool and although she didn't notice herself do it, she took a deep breath before Jude swam to the surface. She watched intently as he took a gulp of air, spinning around quickly to find the side of the pool and rapidly swam to it.

The comfort of the shiny, cold metal bar at the side of the pool was wonderful. Each of the children grabbed it and were each smiling and wiping the water from their eyes.

Vicky watched as Jude wiped the water from his eyes and smiled to his friend next to him. She could see the falseness of Jude's smile, but deep down she knew there was a part of him that was kind of enjoying the lesson.

In the midst of laughter Jude looked up his mother and smiled. Vicky looked down at Jude and gave him a warm motherly smile as well as a small clap of approval. She grabbed her bag, took one more gulp of now cold tea and left the cup and what was left of the bar of chocolate on the bench next to her.

With her bag hanging over her shoulder, she walked up to the top of the balcony and around to the changing rooms where she always met Jude.

'When we get home Jude, I want you to brush your teeth and get ready for bed' Explained Vicky as they drove home from Jude's swimming lesson. 'Dad will come up and tuck you in, okay?' 'Okay mum' Jude said whilst staring at the passing vehicles out of the car window.

On arriving home, Vicky quickly went into the kitchen and poured Jude a small glass of cold milk and grabbed a biscuit from the cupboard. 'Come here Jude, you can have this before you go up and brush your teeth' She said to him before he'd even taken off his shoes. As always Vicky had been on her feet all day and really wanted to grasp at the opportunity to sit down for the first time today and relax in front of the television. She made light work of getting Jude up to bed on "swimming lesson day". The lesson finished at seven o'clock in the evening, which meant that the moment they got in, it was time for Jude to go to bed. His father would take over from where Vicky left off. Ensuring Jude was dressed in his pyjamas and had brushed his teeth. He'd often read to Jude on this particular night and always give Jude the opportunity to ask for one of his favourite books.

Michael walked into Jude's bedroom, placed a few toys on top of Jude's toy trunk, turned off the main light and switched on his small desk lamp. 'Come on Jude' he said impatiently as he waited for Jude to finish brushing his teeth. Jude lied down in bed and listened intently to his father read his favourite book. Michael tucked Jude into bed, kissed his forehead and wished him pleasant dreams.

Michael walked down the stairs and into the

kitchen where he grabbed a bottle of white wine from the fridge, a corkscrew from the draw and two glasses from the cupboard. He poured wine into the glasses and walked into the living room and sat down next to Vicky. 'Long day Vick...' He said whilst handing her a glass and sighing.

Jude rolled over to face the wall and closed his eyes. His nightmares, which now seemed to be a nightly occurrence, were uncontrollable. It didn't matter whether he went to bed on a high or if he had particular thoughts on his mind. He always dreamt about the water, about the people in his dreams and about the discomfort from being away from home.

His body was tired, swimming for Jude was always a gruelling activity, both physically and mentally. Opening his eyes, he rolled over once more and saw the shadows within the darkness of his bedroom and for a split second he was taken back to a memory of his dream. Once again, he closed his eyes and within moments fell into a deep troublesome sleep.

The sea was calm and as the boat slowly rocked from side to side the child could see the horizon moving diagonally, one direction to the next. To most it was an uneasy calm, as if hiding something dark and dangerous. But to the small boy who looked into the deep blue abyss it felt warm. Bright glimmers of sunlight reflecting off the top of the sea, shone up into the eyes of the young boy who was knelt over the side of the boat.

He was bored, the journey had been a long and one which his parents had dragged him on. It felt as if it were their journey and not his and despite this being an adventure, he was feeling both tired and homesick.

With the gentle rocking motion at sea came sickness and it wasn't long before another person had succumbed to sickness. The sound of someone being sick over the side of the boat was uneasy to the child, however he always turned around with his inquisitive mind. He caught the eye of his mother and she beckoned for him to come to her side with a wave of her hand.

The child took a seat next to his mother and she placed an arm over his shoulder.

'You haven't seen your auntie since you were just a baby, I don't suppose you remember her do you?' His mother asked him.

'No I don't, when will we see her?' He asked.

'I haven't seen my sister in six years. We were very close growing up together and would always play together. She and I shared everything and I've longed to meet up with her since the day she left'

'Why did she leave mother?' The boy asked, with a sweet questioning tone to his voice.

'Like many people, to find a better life, to follow her head' She motioned towards her own forehead. 'She didn't go alone, she went with her husband and two children.' She pulled an old crumpled letter from a pocket in her coat and lifted it and started to read.

*"My dear sister I have missed you with all my heart. Not a day goes by to which I don't remember your love and the bond we shared. My only regret, in making the decision to move away, was that I would no longer be near you nor your family. However the need to move my family to a greater place was strong and not a day goes past where I regret the decision I made.*

*The climate here is so changeable. It's hot and dry like home in the summer and cooler and wet in the winter. I even hear there is snow further north and one day we will travel and see with our own eyes.*

*The food is not like home. There are markets and shops filled with produce and providing you have money, there is more food than you could ever imagine. The fruits are so colourful you would not believe your own eyes.*

*There is green everywhere and the water is pure.*

*But it is not home and I still have days where I feel home sick for you, for the mountains and the cattle.*

*I have a job at a shop. I sell clothes to people and the money I earn goes to my family. I wish for you to make the move here. You would love the differences. The people are friendly, difficult sometimes, but in the most part they are friendly. We have lots of friends from both here and home. People who have also made the journey. It was difficult to start with, learning a new language. The children found it easy and spoke it even before myself and Christopher. He says hello and hopes to see you again one day. He has grown fat and soft, but is happy and at ease with his life now"*

The small boy looked up at his mother as she finished reading the letter. There was a small tear which rolled down her cheek and the child lifted his hand and wiped it away from his mother. She looked at him and gave him a huge hug. 'We will meet with my sister soon my son, I can not wait to see her again'

There was an address at the bottom of the letter, a place which she did not recognise and the words seemed alien to her. However she put faith in her sisters written words. She was not one for exaggerating the truth and her request for her family to join her was an honest one.

The child's mother folded the letter back up

and placed it within the envelope it had come. She put the letter back inside her pocket and kissed her son on his cheek. Placing a hand inside her other pocket, she took out a small amount of food which was wrapped tightly in a small towel. She slowly unwrapped the sugary snack, took a small bite herself and handed the rest to her son. 'Eat it my son, you need your strength' She said whilst placing the wrapper back inside her pocket.

The young boy ate the food his mother gave him. It was a sweet sugary snack and as he chewed it, thoughts of home came rushing into his mind. Remaining seated next to his mother, he turned around and stared once more out towards the dark blue of the sea.

# CHAPTER 5

The flight from London Gatwick airport to Barcelona had only been two hours and for Vicky, Michael, Jude and his sister Belle, it had been a quick transit. Door to door the entire journey had taken five hours. By the time they arrived at the cruise liner, they still had four hours before their official boarding time. After the family had checked in their luggage at the airport, the suitcases were sent direct to the ship and further on to their rooms, so they had nothing but their hand luggage to carry on. They all decided to take a walk into town and have a brief look at some of the more local sights of Barcelona. Their cruise would see them going to Italy, Croatia and Greece, so Vicky particularly wanted to see some of Barcelona before they set sail.

With children in tow, both Michael and Vicky held hands as they ventured away from the drop-off area.

'Belle please hold your brothers hand' Vicky huffed as Belle was looking down at her mobile phone. The moment the plane had landed, Belle had turned off the flight mode setting on her phone and started messaging her friends to tell them she'd landed.

Vicky had asked her multiple times to try and engage with the family more this holiday than with her friends via social media. Belle had agreed, but as of the moment, she hadn't given up the habit and was brutally messaging whilst her neck was on a constant tilt downwards.

'Belle come on!' Michael added. 'If we lose Jude even before we get onboard, it'll ruin the holiday for us all' He placed an arm around Belle's shoulder and whispered in her ear. 'It isn't worth the grief from your mum' He said whilst smiling at her.

Belle placed her phone in her pocket and graciously accepted his request.

'Okay dad, but on one condition' She said.

'Oh and what's that? He asked.

'It's that when we get onboard the ship and we're settled. That we head down to the shops and look at a new replacement phone for me. I looked online and they sell the phone I want, twenty percent cheaper than on the high street... It would be a cost saving for you' Despite her desperately trying not to smile, a tiny grin crept from the corner of her mouth and was clearly visible to her father.

'I tell you what Belle. We'll look at the phone when we're on the ship. I'm not promising anything, however the condition will be that if we do buy you one, you don't use your phone every dying moment of the holiday. That you have a break for the duration of the holiday. Is that a deal?' He asked.

'Yes, absolutely' she said with a now massive smile on her face.

'Oh and one more thing, you have to spend some quality time with your brother, mum and I deserve some time to ourselves this holiday'

Belle agreed and was even more excited about getting onboard.

'What have you just agreed to Deal?' Vicky whispered into her husbands ear.

Not wanting to venture too far away from the port, the family headed north up the coastline towards the beaches. They'd look for something to eat and take in the sites and sounds before turning around and heading back.

The children were behaving, all were subconsciously taking it in turns to walk with Jude, who despite his age was walking ahead of them more often that not. They even had to ask him to slow down a few times.

Jude had stopped at a small market stool and was looking at some of the products on sale. The items were laid in lines on the floor and the bright colours caught his attention. Jude played football in a local team and had a few replica football kits at home. So venturing out and seeing the various market stools at the side of the footpath, it was only a matter of time before he found one selling fake replica football shirts. Being they were in Barcelona, there were plenty of people who were selling the shirts of the local world famous football team.

Both Vicky and Michael were desperately trying to keep Jude's eyes away from the shirts and up until this point had succeeded. They'd agreed the moment they spotted the first stool selling the shirts, an hour prior, that Jude already had enough football shirts and they'd buy him something more worthwhile later in the holiday. They also knew that when Jude caught site of something he wanted, it was always a difficult thing prizing him away... in reality they were on borrowed time.

'Dad look, it's the Barcelona football kit!' Jude said.

'I know Jude, it's a nice top isn't it' Michael had long ago realised that by not engaging in conversation, that it was the most effective way of getting Jude off any particular subject. However not wanting to be rude, he often changed his attitude and just commented with closed comments. Not leaving anything open for a further question or comment.

'Can I get one Dad?' Jude asked. The salesman was already holding up a shirt in Jude's size, close to where Jude was standing.

'Come away from there Jude, we're not getting a shirt today.' He said.

The salesman was listening to the conversation and commented in broken English. 'Sir I can do special price for you today. Barcelona is a brilliant team. Twenty five Euro'.

'No thank you' Michael commented, lightly pulling on Jude's arm to prize him away from the market seller.

Before the seller had time to make another comment, Michael had pulled Jude's arm and was walking away holding his hand. He never gave the seller the time of day nor a second glance.

'Why can I not have the shirt Dad? it was only twenty five Euro'

'Twenty five Euro is a lot Jude and you don't have that much spending money on this holiday. Save it until you at least get on the ship. Plus those shirts are made from the cheapest most rubbish materials. It wouldn't last a day before breaking'.

'But we could take it back if it broke' Jude said.

'No we couldn't, those sellers move on every day. It's not like going to a shop in England Jude. These people don't care about what they sell and who they sell to. They take as much money as they can and leave the area. They're all the same… They're con men Jude. Plus did you see how dirty that guy looked, I wouldn't want to buy anything from him anyway. Come on, lets keep walking, I think I see a play park up ahead, over there see, I'll race you'.

Both Michael and Jude ran on ahead of the two girls and straight into the park.

The temperature was hot, but eased with a refreshing breeze coming from the sea. Michael and Jude had been playing on the play equipment for fifteen minutes when Michael went over to Vicky who was sat on a bench next to Belle. She'd bought them all an ice cream and mentioned they should start to take a walk back towards the ship.

'By the time we get back we'll only have an hour and I'm sure they'll let us go on board slightly earlier, come on, let's head back now. I can't wait to get onboard and see our cabin. Plus I'm really hot in these jeans and want to put a skirt on' She said to

Michael.

The four started walking back along the beach front and past the various market stools.

Michael was now in complete holiday mode. No longer was he the formal firm father from home, he was relaxed and ready for a fun holiday. Out of the corner of his eye he spotted something on one of the market stools. 'Guys you carry on walking, I just want to look at something, I'll catch up to you' He motioned for them to continue.

They all looked round at Michael who was now walking back to one of the market stools on the foot path.

He stopped by one of the sellers, who had all his products lined up perfectly organised on the floor.

Michael pointed to a plastic toy phone on the floor. 'Hey, can I just borrow that for a second?' He asked pointing at it.

The seller didn't seem to understand what he was asking and in response told Michael a price for the item. 'Five Euro sir' He told Michael.

'No I don't want to buy it, I just want to show it to my daughter over there' Motioning to Belle, twenty meters away.

The seller still didn't understand and Michael

was beginning to lose faith in his own communication skills. Michael tutted and shook his head. 'Look I'll give you one Euro' He said, whilst now contemplating whether this joke would actually be as funny as he originally thought.

'Three Euro sir' The market seller said.

Being it was only a joke and not particularly wanting to barter, Michael countered his offer. 'Look two Euro?' Michael firmly said. The seller hesitated and sighed, however agreed. He went to place it in a small bag when Michael shook his finger and commented. 'Oh don't bother with the bag, it's not that important' But by that time the item was already in the bag and had practically been handed to Michael.

Again Michael tutted and grabbed the small bag. He picked up his walking pace to catch up to his family who were now all stood by the side of the path watching what he was doing.

The seller looked on at the man who had just purchased the small item. He'd barely sold anything today and hated days like these where no one barely gave him a thank you nor any form of gratitude. He didn't mind doing the work, it was better than some of the jobs he'd don't recently. It was difficult being an African man in a strange city and not fully knowing the language. He was fortunate to have a few friends in Barcelona, people for whom he could trust to communicate on his behalf. They helped him with the necessary things like having a roof over his head at night and finding work. It wasn't the life he expected when he'd arrived in Spain, however it was a better one than the one he'd left behind. With this in mind he never complained, he took it for granted that he was a second class citizen... in fact he expected nothing less here.

He looked at the man rejoin with his family and for a split second he found himself envious of the man's life. Up until this point he'd made a conscious effort to not think about such things. Things that would remind him of the life he didn't have but yet so longed for. To present, he'd done well to focus on the here and now and not at what could have been. However for a brief moment he watched the family laughing and joking at the toy phone their father was thrusting to his daughters ear. He didn't fully understand what they were all laughing at, but he had an idea.

Michael finished with the joke and rested the phone on the bag. Having momentarily taken a seat on a bench, they stood up and continued in the direction they were heading, all still giggling over their fathers joke.

From the corner of his eye, the seller watched as the family stood up and carried on walking away. He noticed the father had left the bag and phone on the bench. He didn't hesitate for one second in walking speedily over to the bench and grabbing the bag. He jogged over to the father and held out his hand.

'Sir' He said politely. 'You left this'.

Michael turned to the seller 'Keep it mate' He flippantly commented whilst waving his hand in a carefree motion.

The seller looked at the bag and casually walked back to his stool. He took the item out of the bag and placed it back next to the other toy phones on the floor. He folded the bag up and placed it with the others.

He vowed to do his utmost to make a better life for himself. He knew the life he wanted wasn't here, working for such people.

# CHAPTER 6

With the arrow pointing in the direction of the hare, Asim knew he had to be precise with his next move. He'd tracked the animal for a short while and after twenty minutes had caught sight of the creature. He knew that Sabrina's father and her younger brother were following, he'd spotted them hunting the same creature. However they were still ten minutes behind him and he'd cleverly covered his own tracks so they wouldn't see his. Asim wasn't being devious, he was being respectful in covering his tracks. He knew full well that Sabrina's father treasured the times he went hunting with his son and it was another huge lesson for the young man to learn. Having such lessons with his father was part of growing up and maturing. It was an important life experience and Asim didn't want to get in the way of it. He just had to stay in front of them and wanted to challenge himself.

Taking aim at the creature, Asim said a quick prayer under his breath for the animal. Then holding his breath and relaxing, he released his grip on the arrow and it sprung out of the bow at an astonishing speed, making barely no sound whatsoever.

Through experience, Asim knew where to aim and that the arrow would kill the animal instantly. However the moment he released it he readied himself to pounce on the creature should it miraculously escape death. It didn't and a split second after the arrow hit its target, Asim was already holding the creature by its hind legs.

He respectfully and carefully placed the animal on the floor and swept his own tracks. He knew the animals tracks would lead both father and son here and he'd be ready to hand them the prize. He'd considered leaving the animal for them to kill, however today wasn't the day for games, the family were all hungry and this large hare would feed them all well.

He hoped to one day make Sabrina his wife and that he would earn the trust and respect from her father. Asim knew it would come in time, but for now, it was time to eat. He crouched and waited for them both to come… he just hoped and trusted that Sabrina's father did not shoot blindly before recognising that he wasn't the prey they were tracking.

The instant the child had thrown the small

rock, Asim had turned towards where it had landed and stepped backwards, out of the shadow and into the view of the boys father. The small child's father had spotted the change in tracks a while back. After a few minutes of tracking, he could see the tracks were periodically changing from a hare to that of something larger. With the clear and certain attempts at trying to hide their tracks, he knew the prey was that of something large and intelligent. The only animal capable of such a thing was a human and the father knew it would be someone from the group. He wasn't annoyed that the prize wasn't what he'd expect, he knew full well that lessons would be learnt from them both and that time away from the group, together, was far more important right now.

'Asim, I knew it was you a while back' The father said whilst dropping his bow and grasping Asim's right forearm in a greeting gesture. The two of them briefly embraced one another then turned to the child.

'Father did you know it was Asim all along?' The child asked.

'I had an idea we were tracking something slightly larger than just a hare. But I wanted you to find the track anomalies also. Did you see anything out of the ordinary my son?'

'I think so father' His expression and description gave the game away.

'I'm not so sure, Asim is a very good tracker and I might add, he is extremely good at covering his tracks.' The father said whilst slapping Asim on the shoulder and smiling at his son. 'Son that is a lesson for you, look for the unexpected and always be prepared for something larger than you're hunting. You never know when something larger has caught your prey before you… Or smaller!' He said whilst throwing his knife to the floor and instantly killing a Scorpion.

'That was amazing!' Asim said whilst standing with his mouth wide open.' How did you even see it in this light? I can barely see my feet.' He said in amazement.

'I heard it Asim.' The father said whilst pointing to his ear and collecting his knife from the floor. 'Scorpions also make for good food. Come, lets head back to camp.'

Walking back to camp, the three walked in unison. The father speaking of his own hunting trips with his father and how he'd learnt some important lessons. Sometimes those lessons were fun and profound, coming from an experience like none other. On other occasions he'd learnt a lesson the hard way, losing a friend to a snake bite when he was the same age as his son.

'There are many lesson's in the wilderness and to be a successful hunter, you must remember them all. They can be the difference between life and death. Regardless of our cattle at home, it is always good to have a backup plan. To be able to hunt your own food is something we should all take as part of everyday life. Your life, your situation can change overnight and you must be prepared for all eventualities... We can all learn something from today'

When they arrived back at camp it was pitch black and the only light came from the many camp fires, spread away from the dusty roadside and into the neighbouring fields. The stars were heavy in the night sky and plentiful, all looking down over the tired travellers. Asim walked into their camp first, he greeted Sabrina and her mother and placed the hare on a rock. He'd already gutted the animal back where they'd caught it and now he quickly prepared it for the fire, everyone was hungry.

The small boy sat down next to his mother who was preparing some vegetables they'd carried with them. She was readying them to boil in the water her husband had returned from the river. He'd brought back a barrel of water and it would be enough to sustain them for a few more days of walking. The small child also had filled some plastic water bottles and placed them next to his mother.

'That looks like it was a successful hunting trip, what did you learn from your father today?' She asked her son. 'Father is a great hunter, he knew Asim was ahead of us the entire time, he tricked us into thinking he might have been larger prey. I learnt that it's important to always be prepared for a larger animal...'

'Or a smaller one' The boys father shouted out from the other side of the fire. He was holding aloft the dead Scorpion which he roasted on a stick and had a number of other dead creatures which he was preparing to roast. No one in the family particularly enjoyed eating such things, however they were high in protein and made for good snacks with a larger meal. Anything he roasted today would look appetising over a fire.

The family all sat together around the orange flames. The crackling of the fire and noises of local dogs and crickets filled the air. It was a warm start to the night. However there were no clouds in the sky to blanket the warmth from the day and it would start to get cold as the hours drew on. Both Sabrina and her mother sat with a sheet around them. Sabrina was close to her mother and she sat with her mothers arm around her shoulder. Neither spoke a word to one another, they sat in the comfort of their own thoughts and enjoyed the peacefulness of the moment. Asim was telling a long joke to the small boy and his father and they continued with more stories of home. The child's father spoke of the many challenges in the world and how they would face their biggest test when they arrived at their destination.

The night was drawing to an end. The family were all tired and the fire had started to die down. Asim stood up and walked off to find some more wood for the fire. With the cool air around them all, they would need the fire to keep warm during the long night.

He came back and carefully placed the logs on the fire. They were heavy, thick logs and would sustain the fire for another few hours. He dropped the remaining logs next to the fire and went and sat down by a tree, overlooking the family huddled round the fire.

The small child's mother lied down next to her husband. 'Asim.' She spoke to her husband. 'Look at him over there.' Asim was bright eyed, sitting under the tree looking over the family and the fire. 'He will make Sabrina a fine husband one day' She said quietly. 'Yes he will. I already think of him as our own son, he also makes me a proud man. Asim will ask me one day for her hand… and I will grant it with open arms. He is a fine man… and a protector.'

The sun arose early and could be seen edging its way upwards from behind the trees. The air was cool and the skies were clear. It was a beautiful morning and the tired travellers were each starting to wake.

'Where's Asim.' Asked Sabrina as she opened her eyes and stood up, looking around them for a sign of him. A lone sheet had been left by the tree he'd been sat under for most of the night and his things were still where he'd left them.

'I don't know Sabrina.' Her father said, now also standing and looking around for him. 'It's unlike him to just get up and go without telling us.'

Suddenly someone could be seen running towards them. The sound of heavy footsteps could be heard before they could make out who it was. It was Asim.

'I have some good news for us all.' He said with his hands on his hips, trying to catch his breath.

'Slow down Asim. slow down' Sabrina's father said, now standing in front of Asim with his hands on his shoulders. 'What is it?' He asked.

'There's word that transport can help us the remainder of the way. It's still a long journey and will cost us money, but it will save us weeks more of walking.' He said with excitement on his face.

They all looked at one another and smiled.

The small boy's mother stood up and looked at her husband.

'God answered my prayers.' She said.

# CHAPTER 7

Vicky was the first of the family to walk the steps leading up to the ship. But instead of excitement at the prospect of an amazing holiday, all she could think about were her chafing legs. She really hadn't thought properly about her attire and after checking-in her suitcase, she'd realised she should have listened to her husband. Step after step her legs literally feeling as if they were on fire.

Arriving at top she was greeted by the Captain of the cruise liner and a few other members of the crew, each dressed in white and looking extremely smart. They greeted Vicky and her family with a warm handshake and wished them a pleasant holiday. Stepping to the right, Vicky was offered a drink from a young woman holding a tray. Vicky went straight for the glass of sparkling wine, as did Michael. Both Belle and Jude were offered a tall glass of orange, which they took with delight. Spotting a neat looking pile of newspapers to the side, Vicky grabbed a copy of the 'Times' newspaper and placed it into her handbag to read later when she had a moment to herself.

'Where are you staying Madam?' Asked a member of the crew. 'I can show you to your room'.

'We've a family suite in... Hold on, I can't remember, let me get my papers from my bag' Vicky explained.

'No, please Madam, allow me to check for you' The young man asked whilst looking on a tablet for where the family were staying. 'Ah lovely, you have a top deck suite. Please follow me.' He said gesturing for them to follow.

The family all followed the young smartly dressed man to their room. He unlocked the door with a card, then handed the card to Vicky. He escorted them in and briefly showed them around.

Standing by the door the young man paused, he wished them a pleasant vacation and smiled at both Vicky and Michael. He'd been told by the more senior members of the crew, that today was "tip day". The day where being extra polite and helpful, as well as smiley, could earn you a few hundred Euros in tips.

But on this occasion, the extra courtesy and big smile had earned him nothing but a slight pat on the back. He turned around and closed the door behind him… then rapidly, but casual looking, walked back to the entrance to the ship to greet some more guests.

On opening the door to their room, they were surprised at what they saw, more so Vicky who'd booked and paid for the trip. It was far more lavish than she'd imagined.

'I know we booked last minute Michael and that we got an amazing deal, but this is something else!' Vicky said whilst walking around the rooms and peeping round into the bathroom. 'It's pure luxury, we paid far far less than we would have had we booked in advance.'

'Without doubt Vick, this was a good idea.' He said as he stood looking out over the balcony. 'Let's get settled in here first, then lets go and have a wonder around the ship and maybe grab something to eat. How does that sound kids?'

'Great Dad, then maybe we can look around the shops also?' Belle answered.

'Yeah yeah Belle, but let's not rush, we have another ten days on this ship.' Michael told Belle, knowing full well what she had in mind.

The family settled into their room. They placed suitcases away on the floor of their own wardrobes, neatly placed clothes within drawers and Jude placed a pair of pyjamas on top of his pillow.

The room was lavish and certainly was a step up in class from their usual holiday. In the past they'd always travelled well. Whether they'd stayed in a tent or in a four star hotel, Vicky always ensured the family had a nice vacation in a good resort. However because she'd left it late in the year to book this vacation, on the advice from a friend, she had found a fantastic package. It was a last minute cancellation and the cruise-liner wanted to fill the rooms rather than have any empty. Although Vicky had known about the high standard of room they'd booked and she'd seen pictures of it online, she simply failed to believe that it would look the same in real life. Kind of like when you see a picture of a burger in an advert but in real life it's half the size and usually resembles something that looks like it was stood on a few days ago.

The room had everything they could possibly want and more. From twin rooms, giving Vicky and Michael the privacy they needed, to the en-suite with jacuzzi and a balcony overlooking the Mediterranean Sea from the very top floor. By no means was it the grandest of suites, but it was certainly up there with the best this cruise-liner had to offer.

Walking out of the room they headed back down the ship, following the signs for entertainment and restaurants. Neither Vicky nor

THE JOURNEY

Michael were particularly bothered about where they went , this was more a reconnaissance mission to see what was around. Everything was included in their package, all drinks, food and entertainment, except for excursions and spending money. Although they were given vouchers to spend in the shops aboard the vessel, a way of getting people into shops and spending their money.

The ship was grand, from the outside looking up at the vessel it was enormous. For a Mediterranean cruise-liner it was one of the largest and most sort after holiday cruises. It had everything onboard that anyone could possibly want. From multiple swimming pools and water slides, to cinema's, bowling allies, crazy golf and even a shopping centre. This was the number one vessel in its fleet and was looked upon as the pride of the Mediterranean Sea.

Walking past the shops, Belle was busying her eyes from side to side, searching for a phone shop. It was here, she just hadn't spotted it yet. But regardless none of the shops were open yet and wouldn't be until they departed from Barcelona. But at least she could get a heads up. Although she wasn't a big spender, it was great looking at all the different clothes shops and big fashion brands. She knew she wouldn't be able to afford many of the items onboard, however it would be nice to look around and dream.

As they continued through the shops they walking up to a large screen displaying the various entertainment facilities on board and for a period, the family stopped. Michael read out some of the evenings entertainment and they took note of what was happening over the coming days.

Up to this point the entire holiday had been all quite overwhelming for Jude. Walking up the gangway leading to the welcoming party when they first boarded the ship, Jude had looked down at the sea. It wasn't a long walk, a mere twenty two meters, however for Jude, that twenty two meters equated to sixty seven steps, and he'd counted each and every one. The sea turning darker with every step he took and with every step forward, it was also a step upward. But other than that and when he'd looked over the balcony with his father, it didn't feel like he was on a boat. There was no rocking from side to side, no noises from waves and no awkward feelings. In fact Jude felt quite at ease for the situation he was in. Walking through the shops he could have been anywhere, all the shops here were much the same as they were on the high street at home.

On hearing his father reading out the entertainment and already knowing what some of the activities were on the ship, he was extremely excited. Especially excited about the crazy golf and bowling, not so much the swimming pools, but certainly the slides. He was also a sociable child and would always talk to other children. Perhaps had he a brother of the same age, then he might not be as sociable. Relying on a brother for company is easy, you always have a play mate around. But a teenage sister who's more into her friends and phone is not quite the same. Other than occasionally playing with his father, Jude would often find himself playing alone in the swimming pool and it would always lead to him finding another child to play with. It just felt like second nature for him to do this. He had a very caring and pleasant side to him and other children would always pick up on this quickly. On many occasions on past holidays he would find himself playing with children from different nationalities, sometimes they would speak English, but in most instances there was a language barrier, however a barrier that would be beaten by the mutual love for a game like hide and seek or tag.

A voice came over the speaker system. It was the captain advising the passengers they would be leaving dock in the next twenty minutes. He pointed out that it was always custom onboard this ship to wave goodbye to people standing on the dock. Families or friends who were leaving loved ones or people just staring in awe at the majestic view of the huge vessel. The family, along with other passengers dotted around, made their way to the left side of the ship.

'Vick there's a bar and observation deck we could head to. Let's get a drink and wave to people from up there' He said pointing at a sign for the bar. He took Jude by the hand and they walked, single file, towards the bar.

Taking a lift up six floors, they exited the lift and straight ahead of them was the bar. Michael led the family into the bar and to his surprise it was fairly empty, other than one other couple sat down in a small balcony alcove overlooking the port. Michael asked what people wanted to drink and told them to go and sit down outside on the balcony. He went to the bar and ordered a round of drinks. Then on a tray he carried them out and placed them on the table. He sat down, placing the tray on a table next to them and looked out over the port.

On the port were a few cars, coaches, taxis and around fifty people staring at the ship. Each looking, pointing and waving occasionally. The family felt like royalty, sitting high above the rest of the ship overlooking the many people standing on deck leant up against the railings. Without notice the captain again came over the speaker system. At first he spoke in Spanish, then English, followed by both French and German. He explained they were about to leave the port of Barcelona and would be sailing up the coast towards France, then out to Sea and along the coastline towards Monaco.

Suddenly, making the family jump, the horn sounded from the top of the ship to signal their departure. Then a moment later they could see the vessel slowly leaving the side of the port. It was a gradual and slow movement, but definite. They all stood up, not noticing the now many guests who'd joined them in the bar area. Michael turned around and noticed at least fifty other passengers were now standing behind them. He turned back around and stared back over the balcony at the people waving to them from the dock.

Vicky wasn't looking at the people down below, she was far more interested in Barcelona. Looking at the many sites she could see from high up on the ship and she felt excitement at the prospect of venturing to the other destinations on their journey.

Jude was looking down at the streets and noticed the park that both him and his father had played in, not hours before. His eyes drew backward and back along the pathway they'd walked. He recognised a few places and could just about make out the man who had tried to sell him a replica football shirt. He looked so small from where Jude was standing, tiny and almost insignificant. Jude noticed the seller was standing alone and watched as he turned around and looked towards the ship. Even from a distance it appeared the man was looking directly at Jude, but it didn't faze him.

For a few short moments, Jude stared at the man... and he wondered whether he felt lonely.

As the seller said goodbye to another lost sales opportunity, he watched as the children skipped away from him, along the path towards the park. It was as if they had nothing to fear in their lives. Everything was just so easy for them. He wished his life would turn around. It wasn't a look that could be seen on his face. There was no sorrow, no frowning nor "down on your luck" grimace that could be seen at all. He hid his feelings deep within his mind. Never once moaning, sulking or letting on to his friends that he felt anything but happiness at being in Europe.

For the most part, he was happy at being in Spain, a new life, new opportunities, but most of all no fighting.

As the horn sounded from the cruise-liner leaving the dock, he turned around. He could see the many passengers on-board and watched as they waved to the onlookers.

'Another one leaving!' He said quietly to himself. There was no jealousy in his tone, but only the thought of what could be, the change in direction and desire for a life he wanted so bad. He turned back around and shuddered. The haunting thoughts of his journey getting here, across the sea from Africa. It was a torrid journey, one which cost him dearly, his life, his family and his home. He shook the thought from his mind. He hated mentally going back there. However being that he worked next to the sea, it was always close to mind.

After making a quick and decisive decision on what they wanted for dinner, the family walked around the ship and back to their room. It had been a long day and the last thing they fancied was a long drawn out three course meal and full evenings entertainment.

The flight out to Barcelona and the waiting around in the heat had warn them all out. And now they'd toured around the ship and had dinner, it was time to get back to the room and relax before their first full day on holiday.

The instant they walked through the door, Belle was already in the bathroom taking off her jewellery and brushing her teeth. She had a quick shower and put her night clothes on. She was the first into bed. It wasn't an odd thing for her to be in bed quickly. She was a straight forward, clear and certain individual and when she'd made her mind up about something, she'd stick to it. Being an early riser, by eight or nine

PM, she was tired and would never stay up just for the sake of it. On sleepovers with friends, she would always be the first to go to sleep and often would be teased by her friends. But she didn't care, she knew what she wanted and tonight it was the comfort of her own bed. Belle said good night to her mother and father, snuggled down into her bed sheets and rolled over.

Jude was quickly into bed after Belle and if she hadn't gone straight into the bathroom and locked the door, he would have been first into bed. Vicky tucked him into bed and gave him a kiss on the forehead. She turned to Belle and wished her a good night, then turned the small light off and shut the door.

'Night Belle!' Jude politely said whilst also snuggling into the comfy bed. 'Good night, don't fart in bed Jude, we both have to share this room for the next ten nights and I don't want it to stink like your bedroom at home.' She said with a tiny hint of humour in her tone.

Jude didn't mind. He wasn't a typical annoying brother, he never made sarcastic comments to his older sister nor did he play tricks on her. In fact, Jude never really did anything with her. The age gap wasn't huge, ten years, however at the age of seventeen, Belle was so against doing anything with Jude, it was literally the last thing on her mind. It always felt like a chore when she had to do anything with him and she made her thoughts well known. But this holiday felt different. She wouldn't go out of her way to play with him, though would take him to a few places and do a few things with him. If it helped in getting her new phone quicker, she'd play with him for an entire day.

Much like Jude and Belle, both Vicky and Michael were also very tired. They'd got ready for bed, having showered and put their night clothes on. Vicky was standing over the balcony looking down and around the ship. It was now dark and she could see the lights from far off Spain. The ship must have been a few miles off the coastline, but the lights from the mainland could still be seen and were quite comforting. It was a beautiful night and warm outside, certainly warm enough for Vicky to only have a silky nightdress on. As Michael approached the balcony he noticed how attractive she looked, standing there on the balcony with the dim light pointing out her best features.

'Look what I found?' He said whilst clinking two Champagne glasses together and placing them both on the balcony table. Michael was also holding a complimentary bottle of Champagne and stood that next to the glasses. He stood behind Vicky and placed his hands on her hips. Then moving his head to the side of her head, he kissed her and rested his head on her shoulders.

'This is going to be a lovely holiday he said, great choice.'

The two of them had a glass of Champagne each then relaxed on the balcony, before checking on the children and heading off to bed.

'Jude's having another one of his nightmares Vic.' Michael said whilst walking into the bedroom.

'Oh, how did you know?'

'He was doing his usual tossing and turning when I walked in. I gently woke him and tucked him in again, he'd pulled the covers right off again.'

'This is becoming a regular thing now isn't it.' She said with a concerned look on her face. 'Maybe we'll see the doctor when we get home, if they persist.'

'I'll talk to him in the morning again Vic, see if there's anything upsetting him. It can't just be about the water!'

Michael got into bed and picked up his book. He always read before falling asleep, he wasn't one for watching anything on TV before closing his eyes, it was a habit from his childhood. He sat upright and started readying under his own small lamp which he shone over the pages of his book.

Vicky had taken the newspaper out from her bag and was looking for something of interest to read. Her eyes were drawn towards an article with a few images surrounding it. Images of African immigrants, all crammed into small boats crossing the Mediterranean Sea to Europe. It was an image which was very well known throughout Europe and there was nothing which the photo didn't describe. The cramped conditions, the small boats and the wake of water left behind by a speeding motor. Without realising the full picture, many peoples views were outlandish, ignorant and unjustified. Their motives for such thoughts were often driven by not reading between the lines and only taking a glimpse at the pictures. The image itself of a prominent wake behind a speeding boat said a lot... Immigrants rapidly coming, to take jobs, to take benefits, to be a nuisance.

'Would you believe this Mike? It's endless, these migrants coming from Africa.' Vicky said with a careless and sharp tone.

'It's immigrants Vic. Migrants move from place to place, immigrants move from country to country.'

'Well whatever, no one's doing anything to stop them. They all come over here, Greece, Italy, Spain, then head on upwards throughout Europe. None of them even appear to have any idea what they're doing or even where they're heading. It's farcical what they're doing. I mean the amount of money Europe's spending on patrolling the coastlines and rescuing these people is ridiculous.'

Vicky carried on reading the article. Tutting, sighing and making her thoughts well known to Michael who was desperately trying to ignore them.

It wasn't long before Michael was fully engrossed in his novel. Despite the constant grumbling, he'd completely switched off from Vicky. What she'd been talking about, the now white background noise, had completely gone over his head.

# CHAPTER 8

The colours of both red and orange swept overhead, bouncing off the few clouds in the sky. It was a glorious end to what had been a long day for the passengers onboard the boat. There were many weary people and most had now relaxed and were silent.

At the start of the voyage there were many men, women and children who were suffering from sea sickness. The images of people heaving overboard and crouching down to their knees was still repeating in the young boys mind. But after a day out at sea, people had started to get used to the constant rocking of the boat and the horizon tilting up and down.

The boy was seated next to a young friend he'd made onboard the boat. Neither child spoke the same language, though they constantly conversed to one another and they both got the gist of what they were saying. Even after a few hours of playing and sitting together, they'd managed to communicate through just simple vocabulary like;

water, sun, pass and their names. His father thought it remarkable and was so proud of his youngest child for being able to communicate in such a way. But most of all he was happy and content the child seamed to only find pleasure in such a situation. Having never been on a boat before and whilst appearing to be afraid of the water whilst boarding, it was clear the trip might be one the child would be troubled with. However up until now there were no apparent signs.

Tossing a small ball from one to the other, the boys took what they could from the situation. It was pretty cramped, however they managed to create their own space for passing the time. At one stage they'd even ventured off on their own for a small period of time. Crawling around the deck, between some of the other passengers. Only in a few instances did they get on other passengers nerves by knocking into people. But for the majority of the time, people were just happy to see two children enjoying themselves. It wasn't until they'd caught the attention of one of the crew, they were told to go back to their parents and sit down. Although yet another strange language was spoken, they understood the threat and distinctive tone in the man's voice, they did what they were asked and sat down next to their parents.

The young boy caught the ball once more,

however he'd had enough of playing for now. The orange and red sky was proving too much for the child and he wanted to look out at the vista. He passed the ball back to his friend and pointed at the sky. He then snuggled into his mothers side and turned his gaze out to the water.

The temperature was still warm from a long hot day and no one was cold. Although the sun was fading, the sky looked hot and intriguing, like it had something to offer. Most of the passengers were now looking up at the sky in awe and were contemplating their next destination and what it would have to offer. The sky had that way of making you feel. As they sat and stared, it made them feel small and insignificant to this world. Each of the passengers believed in some form of heavenly being. A belief was something they each shared and it didn't matter to any of them which God they worshipped. The child noticed that some of the people were kneeling down and praying and he remembered some of his friends from home doing a similar thing.

A small but significant cool breeze swept over the passengers and it took some by surprise. The small boy felt the cool air sweep over his arms, as they hung out over the side of the boat. However the breeze was short lived and no one else thought anything more about it.

The young child could hear people behind him talking about where they were heading and was interested in what they were saying. He turned around as they talked, still sitting tight to his mothers side. His eyes widened and he stared at the people as they spoke.

Even though they were in deep conversation with one another, both men noticed the small child staring at them. It was as if he were prying, trying to obtain some lucrative information to use against them. One of the young men turned and glared at the child, but he did not turn. He was focussed on what they were saying. He didn't recognise either of the men, they were new to him. However they did speak his language and he recognised some of the places they were referring to. One man was speaking of Italy and how he was looking forward to getting off the boat there. The sites of Italy were of course well known around the World, as well as the food and women. They both laughed when the man mentioned about women, but the small child didn't understand why. Listening to the entire conversation, he got the gist of what it was they were talking about and when they started to laugh, he merely smiled in response.

The men both glaring at the small child realised he wasn't going to turn away, so they did. They turned and looked in the other direction and continued on with their conversation.

After a few more minutes the child had lost track of the men's conversation and he turned back around and looked out to sea. The small and out of character breeze from minutes back had developed and the temperature had significantly dropped. Night was staring them in the face as people looked out at the dark clouds developing ahead of them. The sea, though still moderately calm, had developed a slight crest and the boat now moved up and down the crest as it approached the looming clouds in front of them.

The sun was still visible, dipping slightly under the clouds and just above the horizon. It was a devilish sight and the warm orange and red tinge to the sky had gone and was being replaced by a dark blue. There was probably no more than ten minutes of light left in the day and people were starting to talk.

As the child clung to the warmth of his mother, he felt tiredness kicking in. The light rocking of the boat was making him feel drowsy and his eyes closed momentarily. Not wanting to fall asleep he realised he was drowsing and rapidly opened them up again. He rubbed his eyes but remained snuggled into his mothers arms.

'I don't like those clouds ahead of us' The child's

father turned and spoke to his wife. He looked down at his son and saw that he was asleep in his mothers arms. He looked back up at his wife and they looked one another in the eyes. He held out his hand and gripped hers.

The clouds were rapidly forming overhead, then from nowhere a bright light lit a portion of the looming clouds. The child's mother cupped her hands over her sleeping child's ears as he slept and the light was quickly followed by a clap of thunder. A storm was forming ahead of them and the boat was heading straight for it.

Without noticing the incline of the boat, none of the passengers were aware they were approaching the crest of a wave. The noise of the motor was constant, a dull but significant noise the passengers had become used to. As the boat went over the crest of the wave, the motor sped up as it momentarily left the water. The boat crashed back down and with it came a splash of water, covering many of the passengers and waking the small boy.

The child's father grabbed his son and moved him into the corner of the boat and told him to stay down. He then held out his hand for his wife to join them in the corner.

Rain was now falling and there was a constant wind whistling around the boat. The noise of the motor was louder, as if the captain had sped the boat up to get through the storm quicker. There was panic coming from the passengers on the boat. None had expected this to be a long journey, the man ushering them onto the boat had said it would be a few hours. So after a long day at sea and with the conditions worsening, there was no wonder why people were starting to get nervous.

A woman started to cry and despite her husband attempting to quieten her down, she started to wail. The other passengers turned to face her and as they did, the boat jumped once again out of the water. However this time it was harsher.

# CHAPTER 9

'So Belle, it would appear that your choice of a holiday was the right one. I'm so glad you asked for a cruise, this really has been one of my favourite holidays already and we're only a few days into it' Vicky smiled at her daughter.

'Yeah it's been good so far, it's a lot different to how I imagined. I was thinking of taking Jude for a few hours tomorrow so you and dad can have some time to yourselves. Is that okay?'

'That would be lovely, thank you. Where were you thinking of taking him? He really enjoyed the bowling yesterday or there's some films on at the cinema.'

'I was going to take him to the water slides and for a walk around, see what else there's to do, is that okay?'

'Yes it's fine, but you'll have to stick to him like glue the entire time. You can't let him out of sight, not for one second. You know what he's like for wondering off on a whim.'

'Don't worry mum, I know it doesn't seem like I'm responsible, but honest, I'm just as worried as you are when he periodically goes missing.'

'Well I doubt that Belle, but I know what you mean. Yeah that would be lovely.'

'Did you hear that Mike?' Vicky raised her voice so her husband could hear her from inside the bathroom.

'I did, that sounds great Belle, thanks. But what to do with a spare few hours Vic, I'll get thinking.'

'I bet you will.' She said in response, knowing full well what he had in mind.

Michael finished in the bathroom. It had been a long day around the pool and rather than go back to the room to get ready for dinner. They stayed out until late and ate food at the bar area. Although Michael enjoyed swimming, he hated the smell of chlorine and vigorously washed it out of his hair and off his body. He stepped out of the shower, dried and walked out of the bathroom.

'I'm finished Belle if you want to jump in quick.' He motioned for her to use the bathroom.

Michael walked in and saw that Jude was sitting up in bed watching a film on the TV.

'That was a fun day today wasn't it Jude, what did you enjoy the most?' He asked.

'I really liked playing with that boy earlier, his ball was so bouncy.'

'He wasn't English, did you understand anything he was saying?'

'Some things I did, but we mainly just played with the ball. He was nice dad.'

'Yeah, I wonder if we'll see him again this holiday. It's a big boat and people do tend to move from place to place. We'll keep an eye open for him though. Listen, I'll get some clothes on and you can watch TV for another thirty minutes, but then I want it off okay!'

Michael knew full well that Jude wouldn't last any more than another five minutes before he was asleep. He didn't have to worry about Belle watching the television loudly, she would more than likely be on her new phone instead with her headphones on.

Michael walked out of the children's room and back into the main area of their suite. He grabbed his bed shorts and put them on. He towel dried his hair and sat down on a chair and watched whilst Vicky tidied around the place.

'Where's the aftersun cream Vick?' He asked

whilst looking at the redness on his arms.

The weather so far on the holiday had been perfect, no rain, no clouds and one very hot sun. They'd all applied sun cream the entire time they'd been onboard, however the sun had been particularly hot today and Michael had just forgot to apply more cream to his arms. Concentrating more on ensuring both Jude and Belle had creamed up over himself.

It was dark outside, no lights could be seen other that the lights onboard the ship, not even the moon had made an appearance. Because it was dark and had been for an hour, no one had noticed the dark clouds forming over the horizon. The boat was heavy in the water and due to its design, rocked very little. It took a tall wave to rock the boat. However Vicky, who was standing up tidying the suite, noticed as she was casually pulled to the right, then back again to the left.

'Woah.' Vicky said as she moved. It had been the first time on the ship that any of them had felt anything at all. The Mediterranean, up until this point, had been completely still the entire holiday and most people had forgotten they'd even stepped foot onto a boat. The first rocking motion was the first sign they were on a vessel and it would be the first of many that evening.

The speaker system turned on with a beeping noise and the captain made an announcement.

'Good evening ladies and gentlemen, this is your captain speaking. I hope you've had a pleasant day onboard the Royal Jewel of the Mediterranean. We've moved into the path of a storm that's been brewing for a few hours ahead of us. Our satellite weather readings have indicated there are quieter waters north from here, so we'll be heading off course north towards the coast of southern Italy. Unfortunately there's no getting away from this one, however there are calmer waters thirty minutes from here. We've already changed course and you'll notice the vessel rocking less as we move away out of the storms direction. Please bear with us. You will experience some motion for the next twenty to thirty minutes. But rest assured it's nothing that neither myself nor the other members of the crew, as well as this marvellous vessel aren't used to. You will experience a few rocks from side to side, so please do familiarise yourselves, if not already done so, with storm protocol. If you have any questions please note all digital displays will give information and all members of staff will be more than able to answer your questions. I will keep you up to date with both our movements and the storms and wish you a pleasant evening.'

THE JOURNEY

The captain signed off and placed the phone back down onto his console. He then looked at his second in command, the staff captain, and handed over control.

'There you go John, you take us away from this one. It's going to be a choppy half an hour, so some valuable experience for you. Just contact me should the situation change.'

The captain patted the staff captain on his shoulder and walked out, back towards his quarters.

'That all sounds a little concerning Mike, don't you think?' Vicky asked her husband.

'I'm not fussed and from what the captain said, it doesn't sound like a large storm. We'll probably not feel much, his announcement was more than likely just out of protocol and necessity. Don't worry.'

The moment Michael stopped talking, the cruise liner climbed a moderately sized wave. But unlike a small boat, the ship just rolled over the crest and back down the other side. There were no heavy splashes nor heavy jerks, however the majority of passengers noticed something different to what they'd witnessed so far on their cruise.

After hearing the announcement and feeling

the first large movement from the ship, Jude ran out of the bedroom and into the lounge area.

'Dad!' He shouted as he ran in towards his father.

'Don't worry Jude, it's nothing to worry about.' He said with a calming tone.

Jude ran straight to his father's side and sat close to him. 'Will the boat be safe?' He asked with a juvenile concerned tone to his voice.

'Jude seriously don't worry, we'll be out of the storms path within fifteen minutes. It's just normal to have a storm whilst out at sea. Come on, I'll tuck you up tight in your bed and you won't feel anything, you'll be asleep before you know it'

Michael took Jude by the hand and walked him towards his room.

The walk back to Jude's room was slow, methodical and ponderous. The waves hitting the ship's side made for something Jude hoped he wouldn't feel on this holiday. But it was something he feared from the moment the family agreed on where they would be going this year. He just didn't have the nerve to state he hated the sea.

The small child's father sat pinned against that

of his son who was huddled in the corner of the boat. He grasped onto his wife with one hand and a small protruding part of the boat with the other. It was just enough to provide some support and keep him in position as the boat rocked them all back and forth.

Still people were crying, women and children wailed and the rain now heavy, continued to batter down upon them all. One man stood up and fought the wind, rain and turbulence from the boat to make his way to the front where he tried to plead with the captain to do something. As the man approached, one other man stood up and held a gun up to the man. The small boy's father could hear them screaming at one another. The captain was desperately trying to hold his attention on the situation and the worsening conditions. He had little time to be dealing with one of the passengers. looking sideways he watched as his right hand man held a gun to the man and shouted for him to sit down. The man pleaded but it was no use. There was nothing anyone could do to escape the deluge from the storm. The gun was shot in the air and the man shouted for everyone to stay calm and sit down.

The pleading man turned and looked backwards towards where he'd come from. As the rain drenched every part of him he fought with all his might to stay on course, holding onto whatever he could find. Staggering from side to side he either grabbed onto a side rail or someone's head as he struggled to find balance. Suddenly the boat again rose out of the water. The small dim light at the front of the boat, the boats only source of light, shook from side to side, lighting up the rain as it was pushed sideways by the wind. As the boat leapt from the water, the motor screamed in pain, then feeling like minutes, the boat finally crashed back down and the light swung back to the other side. The once pleading man no longer stood nor could be seen. People shouted and screamed, looking over the side of the boat. However all they could see was the pleading man's back, upturned in the water and a split second later he was gone, lost to the sea.

One of the sea's most deadliest of assets is the one that can't be seen. It floats just beneath the surface and can travel thousands of miles if not detected. Just bobbing, slowly moving and waiting for its time to strike. The container from a huge cargo ship had fallen from the vessel weeks back and hadn't been seen. It was floating in the middle of the sea, completely out of sight. With the onset of the storm the container was yanked in every direction, but not once did it falter from its destiny. The twenty foot, steel container was close to air tight and weighing over fifteen tons, it carried as much force as a medieval battering ram.

The small wooden boat stood no chance against the force of the container and the moment the two objects were locked into a collision course, it was only a matter of time before it caused devastation.

As the boat crashed once more back down onto the sea, people were screaming in fright and sheer terror at what was occurring. Then from no where came the sound of crunching, smashing wood as the container impacted with the boat. The sound of panic on the passengers almost came to a halt as people were frantically attempting to work out what was happening, where that noise came from.

The rain and wind continued to plummet down upon everyone onboard and the captain was trying with all his might to gain control over the boat. Still the motor continued, wailing as it struggled to keep up with the heavy demands. The man with the gun, let it go from his hand so it dangled from his shoulder strap and he grabbed the light from above his head. Fighting with the weather conditions and the motion from the boat, he shone it in the direction from where the destructive noise had emanated. A huge hole had appeared in the side of the boat. A hole which had been made by the battering of the fifteen ton container. There was jagged wood protruding from the hole and water could be seen gushing into the boat and then back out again. The entire boat was now engulfed in water and it was only a matter of time before it would completely fall apart, courtesy of the supremacy of the storm.

Passengers were either completely submerged or fighting to restrain themselves. The onslaught of waves pushed and pulled at the helpless people as they crashed all around them. As the young boys mother slipped from the exhausted hands of her husband, the child's last sight of his mother was that of her life being pulled away as she was sucked through the hole in the boat and into the blackness of the sea.

With both hands the young child clutched onto the side of the boat. The wind, rain and waves still battering each and every one of the passengers. The child's father yelled his wife's name as he watched in terror as she was pulled from the boat. There was nothing that could be done for his wife and he felt helpless, more so than ever before in his life.

The boat again jumped from the water, though with the weight of water already on the boat, the jump was far less than before. But it didn't stop the devastation that was to follow. As the boat landed, the weight of water at one end of the boat pulled at every square inch until it was ripped apart.

Screams from every person onboard could be heard over the wind. The motor slowly died and with the end of the boat, sunk deep into the sea. The top half, now a complete wreck, was in bits and people clung on to what they could.

The small child was flung from the boat and crashed into the water along with the debris, the wreckage of the dying boat. He could hear as people cried and screamed over the sound of the storm. The water gushed over the young child, waves and rain still battering the poor boy. And with the onslaught of the storm, he was only able to barely mutter his father's name before another wave crashed into his face.

# CHAPTER 10

### (Two Months Previous)

As the majestic red sun set behind Asim, moments later, his evening prayer was completed. Standing up, he rolled his prayer rug and placed its strap over his shoulder. Then turned to face west where the sun had previously shone. The sky was turning from red to dark blue overhead and within ten minutes it would be dark.

'Are you finished Asim?' His friend asked as he was looking towards the hills.

'Yes Peter, I'm finished. Come on, let's get back now.'

The young men had been friends since childhood and both had turned seventeen only a few months before. Peter's family lived in the same village as Asim's and they were all close friends. Sharing meals together and celebrating special occasions as more like close relatives. The families shared a special bond together. Regardless of their different faiths, their friendship had been long and faithful. They respected one another's beliefs and, as many families in the villages, they enjoyed the company of good friends.

As Asim and Peter walked side by side they both were looking out towards the village. They had spent the afternoon out walking and hunting in the hills and stopped a few times for relaxing, praying and eating. They enjoyed one another's company and were rarely seen alone. Despite Asim being in love with his girlfriend Sabrina, he seemed to spend more time with Peter. Sabrina understood their bond together was strong and she herself wanted her independence. Sabrina was only fifteen years old and potentially they had their entire lives together. Asim was without doubt the one for her. She'd known him for years and despite their different religions, they made their relationship work as so many people in the village did. It was more than common for people of different faiths to mingle and live in close proximity to one another. There were no conflicts, only content happiness and respect. It had been like this for as long as anyone could remember.

'Asim, do you think one day you will marry Sabrina?' Peter asked.

'I do my friend. I think I've known for a long time now that we'll be together for the rest of our lives. It just feels right. But don't worry brother,

I will always have time for you.' Asim said whilst grasping Peter's shoulder.

The sun had well and truly disappeared under the horizon and the dark blue sky had been replaced by black. The stars were fully out and the Milky Way stretched long and far over them. The two young men stopped in their tracks for one last time before they walked down into their village. Asim unrolled his rug and the two men sat side by side. Peter passed Asim his water bottle and Asim took a gulp of water before handing it back to his old friend. They lied down and stared into the night sky. The warmth of the day still in the air, the sound of crickets and other wildlife filling the silence between their thoughts.

'Asim do you believe there's life up there in the stars?' Peter asked questioningly.

'Other than Allah Peter?'

'Yes brother, other than God.'

'I don't know. I believe in Allah and everything in which I'm taught. I've never really given it much thought though. But if God created us, then I suppose they could create other's elsewhere.'

I agree Asim, it's just hard to think that up there, nothing else has been created. The beauty in the night sky is something to truly behold.'

As the two men lied down, they both stared at the stars and for a few minutes said nothing else as their minds raced with multiple possibilities.

In the silence, a faint tone of a vehicle could be heard in the far off distance. There weren't many vehicles around. Only a few people locally, but no one in the village owned one. One of those people being the doctor and the other being some market sellers from a few villages away. But this seemed different, the noise was quickly becoming more noticeable and although still far off, it sounded louder, possibly faster than they'd heard before. Never had they witnessed a vehicle moving as fast as this appeared and it was difficult for them to comprehend what they were hearing. Both men looked around for signs of the vehicle. They knew where the noise was coming from and they were waiting for some sign, maybe the lights of a car or the dust from the only road they knew.

Suddenly they caught sight of the vehicles lights, still at least half a mile away. They couldn't see any dust, being that it was dark, but they could make out the lights and that it was moving quickly through the hills.

'Who do you think it is Asim?' Peter asked with concern.

Sensing this, Asim answered him and tried to give a plausible answer.

'It's probably just the doctor. Maybe there's an emergency in one of the villages. Come, let's try and get down to the road and cut the vehicle off. I wonder what's happened.' Asim said with enthusiasm and excitement.

Both collected their things and started to run in the direction of the road. It was rough underfoot, however being the stars and moon were out and they both knew where they were running, it was fairly easy for them to quickly run without stepping on a rock or tumble head over heels. They could see where they were running and where the road was. The car was sill behind them as they ran down the hill, Peter running behind Asim as they ran in unison towards the dusty road.

The vehicle was travelling quickly, faster than both men had seen a vehicle moving before and they could hear as it approached. It wouldn't be long before they would be down to the road, but if they didn't move faster, they would miss the vehicle as it drove past, leaving them in its dust.

'Quickly Peter, keep up.' Asim shouted as the two men gained in speed. Quickly they approached the road, but just before they got to the roads edge an old rusty truck sped past them.

Packing what they could into the truck, the three men, each in their twenties got in. There were no seatbelts in the truck, only handles to use and the windows had been blown out years ago. This vehicle, though still fast when the peddle was pushed to the ground, had seen better days, however it served it's purpose. With a hard pull and a crunching, grounding thud the men closed the trucks doors. As they set off and pulled round the corner, three people moved in front of the vehicle and the driver quickly slammed on the breaks so as not to run them over.

A man walked to the side of the truck and opened the passenger door and spoke with a harsh "straight to the point" tone.

'Here, take these men with you, they need the experience.' The man in the red cap said whilst gently thrusting two boys into the rear passenger seats.

The boys got in and sat in the back.

There was a long period whilst all passengers were quiet. The three men already in the truck, had not seen these boys before and had nothing to say to them. This was all fairly new to them all, but they had their orders and knew exactly what they had to do.

The road was empty, no one drove during the night and no one would be out on foot in the dark. The road would be completely clear and the driver could manoeuvre the vehicle with ease and without care and attention.

They continued along the dirty road to the third village they would come to. It would be a long drive, possibly half an hour through the hills. But with the drivers foot heavy on the peddle, the journey wouldn't take too long. And for the passengers, it would be a journey they would enjoy… if not a little apprehensive of their orders.

As Peter and Asim reached the road, they stopped exactly behind where the truck and driven seconds before. As they stopped they both felt fatigue and rested with their hands on their hips, panting, attempting to catch their breath. They looked up at the vehicle, not fifty meters away and saw two red lights brighten, then the vehicle quickly came to a halt. A huge clunking noise came from the change of gears and the truck reversed quickly and clumsily towards the two young men. Stopping just before their feet.

'Quick, get out you lot.' The driver said to the others in the truck, who'd noticed the two young men running down the hill and onto the road behind them.

They all got out of the truck and stood in front of Asim and Peter. The driver of the vehicle looked into the rear view mirror at his reflection in the dim light, then grabbed something from his side. He got out, slammed the truck door closed and casually walked from the other side of the vehicle. Peter could see as the man got out and as he walked around the back of the car, he saw the man was holding a large gun in his hands. Peter looked at the weapon in shock and tugged at Asim's arm. The man walked in front of the other people from within the vehicle and stood in front of Asim and Peter.

'So where are you boys going?' He asked in a rough, sharp tone, looking at both Asim and Peter.

'Back home. Why were you driving so fast, where are you going?' Asim asked in response.

'I'll ask the questions boy!' Again speaking sharply. Regardless of the age difference only being five or so years, the driver felt powerful and in control of the situation whilst he held the gun. He called Asim boy in the hope of obtaining a form of parental respect and it worked. It shut Asim and

Peter down and they were at the mercy of the men standing in front of them.

'What do you want?' Asked Peter, who was clearly shaken.

'We're recruiting soldiers to fight with us against the Government.' The driver said

'You don't look like soldiers!' Asim said.

One of the other men stepped forward and punched Asim in the face. It startled Asim more than hurt him. He wasn't knocked to the floor, he merely raised his hand and felt his chin where it had been struck. 'Sorry, I didn't mean any disrespect. It's merely an observation as you're not wearing a uniform.' He said whilst looking at the two young boys standing next to them.

The driver raised his gun to Asim and fired it so the bullet shot passed his ear.'There, is that confirmation for you that we are soldiers?' He again said cold and sharply.

'We're not soldiers and we've no interest in joining, I'm sorry. There's villages further over the hills, you could try there, but I don't know if you'll get any luck. We're all farmers, hunters and craftsmen here and wouldn't be any help to you brave men. Asim spoke, still rubbing his jaw and now in obvious shock at the situation. However he stood his ground and tried desperately to hold his tongue and nerve.

The driver laughed at Asim and the other people from the truck joined in. The two boys who'd gotten into the truck last had no real comprehension of what it was they were laughing at. However it made them feel big and supportive of the driver. So they joined in the laughter and stopped when the driver did.

'You don't understand boys.' The driver said. 'I'm not asking people if they'll join us, I'm telling you that you'll join us.'

On hearing this, Asim looked around at the other people from within the truck. No one seemed to have any other weapon, it was only the driver. Asim saw no other way around the situation. The moment the driver wasn't looking at them, Asim pounced and fought for both his and Peters life. The purpose of his attack was to grab the gun and then rather than fire it, he'd use it to get themselves out of the situation.

Asim grabbed at the gun with one hand and punched the man in the face. The gun was ripped from the man's hand and was thrown to the floor away from the people and the truck. Asim continued his attack whilst Peter, still not knowing what to do, stood there for a moment and watched as the fight started. Asim threw one more punch, then looked for where the gun had fallen. The other men, who'd been stood behind the driver weren't expecting this retaliation and like Peter, were taken by surprise. Before they knew what was happening, Asim had already disabled the gun from the driver and was in the process of leaping towards the weapon which was still out of his reach. As Asim was preparing to leap for the gun on the floor, the driver had picked himself up and was also attempting to get the gun himself. Then without notice one of the young children pulled a gun from their waist and fired it towards Asim. Although it was aimed at him, it missed him and only acted as a deterrent, a warning shot, rather than the deadliest force it was meant.

Shaking after pulling the trigger, the child just stood there, still pointing the gun at Asim. Asim had now turned around, having not made it to the gun on the floor in time. The driver walked over to the child and took his gun from his hand, without any persuasion. Holding the gun in Asim's direction, he looked at the boy who'd fired the gun and patted him on the shoulder. He then walked over to Asim and this time, with the butt of the handgun, jabbed it at the side of Asim's face. Asim was forced to the ground. Peter was watching the situation unfold and felt completely helpless. he'd never once been in a situation of this nature and was completely shocked, still and silent. He watched as Asim was forced to the ground and watched as the driver held the gun to his head in an assassination pose.

'No!' Cried Peter, 'Please stop.'

The driver turned towards Peter, still holding the gun to Asim who was kneeling on the floor by the drivers knees.

'You.' He said to Peter. 'You get in the truck, you will fight with us... or I'll kill your Muslim friend.'

Peter looked at Asim, a tear rolled down his cheek. There was absolutely nothing he could do, he was in a no win situation. To think that only minutes ago they were running, feeling excitement at seeing a vehicle driving so fast. And now, the situation has been completely turned upside down and is one of sheer terror.

Peter, still looking at Asim, whispered the last words he'd ever say to his friend. 'I'm sorry brother.' He then dropped his shoulder and walked towards the truck.

Asim couldn't believe what was happening. He knelt there completely helpless, watching his best friend, his brother, walking away from him and there was nothing he could do which wouldn't cost him his life. He knelt there and with gritted teeth said nothing.

One of the other men picked up the weapon

from the ground and held it aloft. The driver asked him to stand by Asim and make sure he doesn't do anything stupid. He then told the other three people to get in the truck. The driver looked at Asim, his cold dark eyes piercing a hole straight through Asim.

'Your friend is very brave, Muslim. I've spared you this time as I myself follow Islam. But I might not spare you next time. If I see you again, you will come with me.' He gave Asim one more stare, then turned and walked back to the truck. He got in, slammed the old door and turned the key to start the engine. He turned the truck around and drove in the direction from where they'd come, leaving both Asim and the man with the gun standing in the middle of the dusty road.

The truck stopped, not twenty meters away from where the two men stood. All Asim could hear was the sound of the old engine rattling away and the lights from the old truck were lighting up only the road ahead of them. The red tail lights were lighting up a small area from behind the vehicle and dust blew past the truck as it ground to a halt. The man with the gun dropped it from its raised position and he ran towards the vehicle, jumping into the rear. The driver took one final glimpse at Asim and put his foot down and accelerated away.

Asim, now standing alone in the darkness

watched as his friend disappeared into the darkness of the night.. and with it their long brotherly friendship disappeared.

# CHAPTER 11

The nights sky had formed over the families heads as they sat and conversed around the newly lit fire. Jokes, tails and a small amount of gossip filled the air as the two families enjoyed each other's company. It was never the plan to get together on this particular night, like so many times, one minute they were in their own homes and the next they were already gathering together. It was common for the two families to get together

Sabrina was sitting next to her brother and rather than engaging in conversation, she was eagerly awaiting for Asim to walk around the corner. It was unlike him to be later than normal. Due to his prayer, his life was such a routine, occupied by religion, work and education. He'd said to her that he and Peter would make it back for just after sunset and that he would share the evening with her. It was now almost an hour after the sun had set and she was starting to feel restless, as if perhaps something untoward had occurred.

'Sabrina you look worried.' Her mother called

out from the other side of the fire.

'I'm not mother, I'm just wondering where Asim is, he said he'd be back shortly after sunset.'

'I'm sure he'll be back soon, he's probably just strolling back now.' By pure coincidence, she spotted Asim in the corner of her eye. 'Look, there he is!' Sabrina's mother said looking across the land. Asim was fifty or so meters away, slowly walking with his shoulders slumped.

'There is something wrong mother, where's Peter?' Sabrina stood up and ran towards Asim.

'Asim!' She shouted as she ran full pelt towards him.

Asim was now standing in the middle of the dusty road, watching as his friend had been taken away. The red lights on the truck were quickly fading away in the opposite direction and with it the noise of the old, tired engine quietened. It would be the last time he saw his closest friend.

Tears now rolled down his face as the reality of the situation came to fruition. And the understanding that he could do nothing weighed down heavily upon his shoulders. After a few moments of shock and despair, Asim picked himself up and started thinking what he could do next.

There would be no use in following the vehicle, it was already too far gone. It would take him hours to catch up with it. if indeed he could ever find the truck. After all he had no idea where it was heading nor who those men were. There was simply nothing else he could do other than walk back home. Asim started to jog, however he thought about it and realised there was no vehicle in the village. No one would want to go out in the darkness to search for Peter, it would have to wait until the morning, regardless of the dire situation at hand. And the moment those thoughts entered into his mind, he stopped jogging and walked. Shoulders slumped, head down and tears weeping from his eyes. It felt like his world had collapsed and that nothing again would be the same.

As Sabrina shouted his name, Asim's head rose and he ran towards his girlfriend.

'Where's Peter?' She asked in surprise at him not being there, hoping that he'd gone a longer route or stopped off somewhere.

'They took him.' Asim said in response.

'Where, who took him?' She asked, feeling a sense of concern sweeping over her.

'Men in a truck came, they stopped us on the road side, they had guns, Peter had to go.'

'Hold on Asim you're not making sense, slow down my love, what happened?'

Asim explained what had happened on the roadside as they stood in the field opposite their home. The people around the fire each intrigued by what Sabrina and Asim were talking about. Sabrina's father, Jonathon, stood up and walked over to her side. After Asim had again explained what had happened, Jonathon took Asim, with an arm over his shoulder and they walked back to the fire.

'What's happened?' Asim's father looked at the despair on his son's face. He stood up and confronted his son. 'My son, where is Peter?'

'Some men came, they said they were soldiers and that we had to go with them to help fight against the Government. I explained that we weren't soldiers and that no one in any of the nearby villages would be good fighters, but they didn't listen. I tried to fight them, but they had guns, there was nothing I could do. They were going to shoot me and told Peter to go with them or they would kill me. They said they would spare me this time because of Islam and that they would come again and when they did, I would have to go.' Asim spoke quickly, like he was trying to divulge everything on his mind before he forgot anything of importance.

Asim looked at his father. 'We have to go and tell Peter's parents what's happened, I don't know what I'll say to them, he could even be dead now...' Asim's father placed a hand on his son's chest. 'Stop Asim, stop. Come, we will go together and I will tell them.'

Sabrina's father Jonathon, stood up and walked with his friend and Asim, they would go and speak with Peter's father and discuss what their next move would be.

The following day started like any other. The sun waking up just over the mountains and casting deep and long shadows over the village. To merely look up into the hills and distant mountains, as the sun was rising, was difficult and blinding. The sun's rays piercing through the air, lighting up insects, dust and the group of men following the road east to where Peter had been taken.

The moment news spread around the small village of Peter's disappearance, a group of men, including Asim assembled. They would not be going to the site to wreak havoc or to fight, they simply wanted to retrieve Peter and bring him home. There was no uncertain person within the village, this was something they all knew was necessary and something they all one hundred percent agreed with.

# THE JOURNEY

There had been talk over the previous six months that something was happening on the other side of the hills. However up until now, nothing had happened and the only sign of anything untoward was that of whispers, a little gossip or news from another distant village. No sign of danger, no sign of militia nor turmoil had occurred. The news of Peter's disappearance had come as a surprise to everyone in the village. But they decided they would be the first to see what was happening. Their aim was to walk to where ever it was Peter was being held and to take him home. However the villagers were not used to violence, they had no guns, only a few people with bows and arrows and hunting knives. And those weren't meant for violence, only hunting. They had no idea how long the journey would be, however they assumed it would be at least half a days walk. The whispers around the village over the previous six months, were of a small force of men, no longer tolerant of the Government, who wanted to upset and disrupt the politicians into making changes that would benefit them. There was talk of some kind of compound attached to a village ten to fifteen kilometres away, but no certainty, only talk. The way the villagers saw it, was that this was a mistake, that Peter was taken as perhaps a misidentification or something of that nature. Peter wasn't a fighter, he was clever, a young potential tradesman who would one day help the village in modern ways in which no other person had been able to in the past. They wanted him back, they needed him back and they were ready to bargain for his return.

The modest band of men had been walking for the majority of the morning. They'd passed through a small village known to them and asked if they'd heard of any dangers along their path. People seemed to be quiet, as though they were fearful of talking. Although none openly said there was anything untoward going on, it was obvious they wanted to talk and disclose information. But all the band of men could obtain was there was perhaps uncertainty in the next village. But what that uncertainty was, they couldn't grasp. They had no choice but to go there and find out for themselves. Though a little apprehensive about the situation, they continued, however they continued in a more regimented and orchestrated fashion. Looking around them for signs, sending one man ahead and being ready for whatever they may find. Extra caution and vigilance was all they could do.

It didn't take them long to come across the village, or what was left of the village. Hiding from site on the top of an overlooking hill. The band of men looked over what they remembered as a happy village, only now there was turmoil and destruction. A few of the men had been to the village years back, but because of the distance and due to there being no specific reasons to go there, none had ventured in that direction for some time. To see a village completely desolate of people and homes destroyed was concerning and upsetting. To the north of the village there was a small compound and people could be seen taking aim at targets. Suddenly a shot was fired, then more followed as the other fighters took aim at the targets. A taller man in a camouflage top could be seen organising people and it was clear that he must have been a leader of some kind.

Asim looked at his father, hoping for an answer of some kind. However no man had any answer nor knew what could be done. None had seen anything like this before, they'd never been in a situation of this magnitude, none had even seen a gun up close.

'What can we do?' Asked Asim to the men on the hill, expecting someone to say something useful.

'I don't know Asim, what can we do?' Peter's father said in response.

'Well we have to do something, Peter is down there somewhere and we can't just leave here without him... or at least try talking to someone there.'

Before anyone could say another word,

Jonathon started to walk down the hill towards the compound. He was brave, though most thought him somewhat reckless on occasions, acting on a whim rather than thinking things over. But mostly his decisiveness had paid off in the past. It wasn't a surprise to see him walking towards danger, rather than staying away and this was why he was the most successful hunter in all the local villages. Jonathon had the ability to think things over quickly, methodically and rationally. He didn't mind people thinking he was rash in his decisions, as long as his success rate was up, then people couldn't question him. Before long, the other men had joined him on his walk towards the compound. They didn't know what Jonathon's plan was when he got there, but they trusted him and hoped he had the answers.

As they staggered down the hill towards the compound, Jonathon looked back at Asim and told him to go back to the top. He knew the men who'd threatened him the previous day would recognise him and it would be dangerous for him to be there. Jonathon knew it was for the best that Asim keep his distance, this was potentially a time for maturity and wise thinking, not for youthful ignorance and rash thinking.

Asim moved back to the top of the hill, keeping out of view from the compound below, but still being able to keep an eye on events. He sat on a rock and looked over the men traversing the rocky terrain, wishing he could have gone with them but equally respecting the word of Sabrina's father Jonathon.

Asim watched as the men moved closer, edging their way down the hill, walking around large rocks and kicking up dust from the floor. They were close now, no more than a hundred meters from the large metal gate.

Suddenly came a few shouts from the compound and people were running towards the gate with their guns raised. The men had been spotted.

Asim sat there on the rock watching intently as the situation unfolded in front of him. He was agitated, his pulse was racing, he was breathing heavily and his hands were twitchy. The thought of going down there in support of his fellow villagers came over him. However he was intent on staying put, realising there was no use in going down as it could put him or the others in danger. He only hoped they would be able to reason with the people and get Peter back.

Asim watched as the men arrived at the entrance just as the men with guns also arrived simultaneously.

'What do you want?' Brutally asked one of the men at the gate.

'Who's in charge here?' Asked Jonathon, standing upright and as tall as he could in front of the group of men.

'What does it matter to you old man, go back home.' Shouted the young man, partially spitting in the face of Jonathon as he spoke with such emotion and anger.

Pushing the small crowd of men to one side as he walked through, came the leader of the group, or General, as he liked to be referred. He pushed his way forward and as he approached the front gate, men stood to the side to allow him to speak.

'I'm in charge here, these are my men, my soldiers. What do you want?' He asked less aggressively than the first man.

Asim still watching the episode unfold, still remained on edge the entire time. He couldn't hear what was going on, only the occasional shout from one of the soldiers. He clung onto his hunting knife, regardless of the fact he never intended to use it. However it made him feel more comfortable knowing his trusty knife was near.

Out of the corner of his eye he saw as a younger

man, a few hundred meters from the rest drop his weapon and start to walk over to the gate, it was Peter.

Peter had been with some other young men, forced to fire bullets at targets. With no hope of escape and seemingly no other options, he'd listened to what he'd been told by the General. By no means had he been brainwashed in such a short amount of time. Though Peter had decided it was far the better option to stay put and do as instructed until some form of opportunity arose where he could escape.

After being given a small but modest breakfast, he tried to make conversation with some of the other men and children in the compound, but none offered any form of conversation other than regarding what they would be doing today. It was as if they'd been instructed to never talk about home or how they came to be here. Peter was shocked beyond belief, he had no idea whatsoever this place was even here… or that there was even such a place on Earth. There was nothing further he could do, but try to not think of home or his family and go with the flow. It would be the only way he could get through this ordeal.

Peter noticed some men had run towards the gate and he caught sight of perhaps someone he knew. 'Could it be his friends and family had tried to mount some form of an escape for him?' He asked himself in that brief moment he saw the people at the gate. However they were a few hundred yards away and he couldn't quite make out who was there and what was going on. Then as Peter saw the General approaching the gate, a space cleared and he caught a glimpse of his father and Sabrina's father Jonathon.

Without hesitation Peter dropped his gun and started to walk, then jog, then sprint to the gate. He never once thought about what he was doing nor even listened to the man in charge of the firing range shout for him to stop.

As the man shouted at Peter to stop, the General and a few others from the group of men heard and turned around. They watched as the new recruit ran towards them at the front gate. 'Father!' He shouted as he neared the entrance and in response, on seeing his son, he shouted for Peter, nudging himself forward in front of Jonathon. As Peter neared the gate, the General aggressively moved a small child aside, no more than ten years of age, with one brush of his arm. He pulled a small handgun from his side and never for one moment hesitated to pull the trigger.

Asim watched in terror as he spotted his old friend running to the front gate and watched as he was struck down by the first of two bullets, then a split second later came the deafening sound of the shots, echoing through the hills around him. Asim gasped in disbelief as he saw his friend gunned down and could do nothing to help.

'My son!' Peter's father shouted as he clung onto the tall rusty gate, trying desperately to get inside. He grasped one hand through the bars, thrusting it inwards towards where his son lye dead on the floor.

The General raised his gun and aimed it at Peter's father, through the gate. Tears rolled down his face as he stared directly through the General, not giving him a moment of his attention, he never even noticed the man holding a gun to his head.

'Hey!' Shouted the General to Peter's father. He was brought back to the moment and looked the General in his eyes. 'Why?' He asked.

'Because I can and because I am in charge here. He will set a good example to the rest of the soldiers here, this is why. Now go, get out of here before I shoot you all.' He shot his gun in the air until there remained no other loaded bullets. He then looked at Jonathon. 'Now get out of here before I reload my gun and shoot the contents at you all.'

Jonathon knew what to do, there was to be no gambling on this man's word. They would have to go and find help some other way. Peter was dead, there was no more they could do today. They had no other options but to quickly disperse. Jonathon turned to the other men, he lowered his head and gestured for the men to follow. They all turned and started walking back up the hill, other than Peter's father who still stood at the gate. As the General placed bullets back into his handgun he never noticed as Peter's father drew his hunting knife from his side. Within a split second he'd drawn it and thrust it towards the head of the man who'd murdered his son. But, before it struck him, the young child who'd been pushed aside before shots had been fired at Peter, reacted in a way of that of a righteous hero. He raised his hands and did what he could to get between the blade and the General.

As Peter's father's blade moved violently towards its target, the child's arm got in its way. The General who'd finished reloading his gun, placed the clip back into place and saw only a quick movement from the child standing to his right. He and many other people standing at the gate, were caught completely unaware by the actions of the man with the knife. To the General, it felt as if the moment lasted forever, even the sound around him seemed to dull as the child flung his arms over his head. The General watched as the young child fell, then stood up in delight at what he'd accomplished. The whole thing happened so quickly, the child never noticed the pain as the knife slashed at his wrist, cutting his artery and allowing him to bleed profusely. He clutched at his wrist and dropped to the floor as he caught sight of the blood protruding with such speed.

The General again raised his gun in the direction of the man at the gate and shot him, point blank in the forehead. There was no missing and no questioning himself. It was the first and only thing that entered his mind. He then turned and looked at the child on the floor. 'Thank you soldier.' He said as he looked down at the boy. He then shouted for someone to come over quickly and tend to the child on the floor. But it was too late. No one had thought to attempt to stop the bleeding, most were in shock at what had happened and none had ever seen such an injury. As the only person in charge of first aid approached, the young child was already starting to fall asleep. Other than the smile on his face when he'd realised he'd saved the life of his General, he never made another sound, no shout, no scream, no quiver of terror. Any childish attributes had been drained from him over the past year he'd been in the compound and before anyone could help him it was already too late. His breathing slowed to a complete stop and his eyes glazed over, he laid completely motionless, dead on the floor.

Jonathon stopped when he heard the shot fired,

fearing the worst he turned and watched his friend, Peter's father, lying on the floor by the gate. He turned back around and continued to run with the other men up the hill towards an onlooking Asim.

'Shall we go after them General?' Asked one of the soldiers, who was standing looking down at the dead child.

'No, leave them. I know where they come from and where they will be. Their time will come...'

# CHAPTER 12

The mood of the men, whilst walking back to the village was sombre, extreme shock and of a complete lack of hope. They'd been taken by surprise at the compound and had been completely unprepared for the situation that had occurred. No one could have guessed the situation which unfolded in front of them, none had ever witnessed anything like that in all their lives and equally none had heard there was a small militia gaining in size… and with such hatred and anger at the helm. They were a peaceful community, living in harmony with one another and other local communities.

After they had reached the onlooking Asim, Jonathon had looked back at the compound, almost fearing what he would find. He hoped they would not make chase, come after them with their guns. They would have absolutely no hope fighting in a small battle with these men and their guns. As Jonathon turned, he watched as the compound went back to their daily routine, leaving the bodies of Peter and his father laying on the ground with no compassion and no respect. He thought to himself that surely they wouldn't leave them there all day, no one could be that full of hatred. But most of all he saw no signs of people coming up the hill after them. Allowing the men to continue their walk back home, Jonathon stayed behind, out of sight from the compound, but able to keep an eye on what they were doing, hoping beyond belief they would not pursue the small band of men. Jonathon waited for a few hours, keeping a watchful eye on what was happening.

Some of the men continued firing their weapons at the targets and some were walking from building to building. However from the distance Jonathon was watching, he couldn't quite tell what they were up to. But whatever it was, it looked concerning and would be something that could affect not only their own village, but other villages in the area. After a few more hours, two men collected the dead bodies of Peter and his father. Jonathon was more at ease for that small detail and a small part of him felt relieved they hadn't been left to rot. After watching the men disrespectfully dump the bodies together on the floor, Jonathon decided there was nothing more to be gained by waiting around and he was conscious of the hours of daylight remaining. He momentarily closed his eyes, collected his thoughts and stood up. Taking one final look he watched in disgust as one man doused the two dead bodies with petrol from a small can. Then with the strike of a match, ferocious flames arose from no where and with it, Jonathon quickly turned around and started his walk back to the village. The haunting vision of the flames rising from the bodies was one he would struggle to rid himself of.

The following few days had been awful at the village. There was a huge sense of anger amongst all the villagers and on the few occasions where people had talked about possible solutions, nothing tangible had been suggested. The local Police had nothing to add, except to say they would look further into it. However their lack of empathy and apparent lack of interest was met with angry defiance from the those who reported the crimes. It was almost as if the police knew what was happening and equally knew they could do nothing to stop it.

Taking a seat within the circle of friends in the local school, Jonathon nudged his rusty metal chair forward. It made a screech noise on the floor and a few people turned to look at him. He smiled in response and decided to stand up and address the floor.

'What has happened to our village is a disgrace. Our friends have been taken from us and murdered, the police will do nothing to help us and I feel our freedom is under jeopardy. We have no way to fight back and to be honest, despite what has happened, I don't want to fight back, too much blood has been spilled already and I don't want anyone else needlessly getting killed. We are a friendly village, none of us deserve this in our lives. We need to decide what to do, we need help from somewhere, but who can we turn to? We come here tonight to discuss what our next move needs to be. Do we fight for our freedom, for our children's freedom and risk our lives in doing so? Do we harass the police into doing something? What are our options here, where else can we turn?'

Jonathon slumped back down on his chair, his head dropped and he faced the floor. For someone who was known locally for being wise, for having the answers to peoples problems, he was completely downtrodden and exhausted. The lack of sleep he'd had in the last few nights and the constant worry of the future was draped over his shoulders. Whenever he closed his eyes he was reminded of the two burning bodies from the compound. Whenever he reopened his eyes, he found himself questioning his actions. Was he right to boldly go down the hill to the compound? Should he have foreseen the events and made Peter's father stay behind? His actions ran through him like a dark cloud hanging over his soul and for the first time in a long time, he found himself wanting to look to someone else for the answers. He no longer had the desire to be a focal point in the community. Any thought he'd had to help lead these people, his friends, had been lost the moment he turned his back on the entrance to the compound. The moment he felt so helpless when hearing the shots fired that murdered Peter's father. From that instant, Jonathon felt like he had no respect, no answers and no rightful justification to be that focal point people turned to.

On dropping his head, people could see that Jonathon was down. They all were down, no one had the answers and with the murder of their friends, everyone felt like they'd lost a relative. The shock of the deaths had hit the villagers hard and was a complete shock.

One man called out to Jonathon from the other side of the room. Not a close friend of Jonathon's, but someone whom had previous looked up to him and had gone on the trip to Find Peter. 'What were you thinking when you went down that hill on your own, brash and bold like a bull?' He said, pointing at Jonathon.

Jonathon looked up from the floor and could think of nothing to say in response. Now it was the turn of his friends to question what his motives were. He'd already punished himself, but now the people were questioning him, he felt completely and utterly lost for words. The dark cloud again rose over his head and he felt the weight of the world on his shoulders.

Another man stood up and addressed the person who'd questioned Jonathon's actions.

'Come on Asif, my friend, this wasn't Jonathon's fault. None of us had the answers on that hill and let's be honest with ourselves, being the police don't seem to be taking this seriously, our only option was to go down there and see for ourselves. Jonathon was simply the first person to go down that hill. It could have been any of us, he was simply the first. The events that followed, Peter's running for the gate and Christopher's reaction to his oncoming son, no one could have predicted that and no one could have done anything to stop their reaction. Placing the blame, or even questioning our friend is not the way forward. Jonathon, things happen for a reason, sometimes things happen and they're out of your control. This was not your fault, we need you right now, we need you to help us find a solution. Hanging your head and feeling shame, guilt or whatever you are feeling right now, will not help us. Please, hold your head up my friend, you are not at fault here, you're probably the bravest of all of us.'

Jonathon raised his head, he silently muttered thank you to his friend and looked back around the room for another source of inspiration. Perhaps someone else would have an answer, but people were looking around the room just as much, hoping someone else would say something. Then Jonathon stood, he had no real idea of what he was going to say. He only hoped that something would arise in his head when he stood up.

'I think we need to get the police in here. We need to speak to them as a group, vent our anger at them as a collective and hope they can do something. If they can't do something themselves, then perhaps they can call someone who can. I mean this is in their interests right?

People nodded in unison and agreed that Jonathon was right, speaking singly to the police may not be enough, but together, they might just have enough to push them into doing something.

It was late in the afternoon and people were restless, Jonathon proposed they speak to the local police Chief that evening and pressurise him into doing something. The Police station was more a small rundown building in one of the adjoining villages an hour away. He opted to walk there and request the Chief go back with him to the village, to meet with the people collectively. A couple of other men offered to go with Jonathon, showing their loyalty towards him. Jonathon thanked the men and they walked out the school and along the path to the next village.

The three men walked into the old white police station. It wasn't in good condition, the doors were falling apart and the whole place needed repainting. There was one cell in the corner of the single story building, however it was dusty, unused and had rusty bars. It had been years since anyone had been in there. The Police Chief was sitting at his desk and as the three men entered, he tried to make himself look busy. He immediately sat upright and readied some papers in front of him.

'Yes, how can I help you?' The Chief said. As the men had entered the building, the light from outside pierced in and with it the dust in the air hid the faces of the incoming men so the Chief couldn't make out who had entered. When he saw Jonathon had come back again and that he'd brought company, he didn't even bother to hide his deeply frustrated sigh. He thought he'd dealt with this situation the previous day. He'd told Jonathon that he would make enquiries and that he'd let them know in due course if he could do anything. But given the situation and the rumours surrounding a militia compound and that those roamers were gaining traction, he really didn't want to get involved. Especially if there was the potential of danger, of repercussions. He wasn't used to danger, being the police Chief around these parts was one of the simplest jobs you could have. There was no crime in the area, no thefts, nothing. The most he ever got involved in was a missing person, who more than often turned up a day later or when he had to take someone to see a doctor in an emergency. It was a simple job that required the right sort of person. And Chief Gabir was the perfect candidate for the post.

'Oh it's you again Jonathon. I told you yesterday that I would look into this. You have to leave me to my investigation.' He said, looking Jonathon in the eye.

'And what have you done today Chief Gabir? You haven't been to see the grieving widow and mother, nor have you spoken with Asim who was with Peter the night before. What have you done?' Jonathon asked.

'I have spoken with other Chief's in the area to see what they've heard about this compound you mentioned. But I'm not really hearing anything out of the ordinary.'

The Chief hadn't made any calls during the day. The concern he had with risking his own life in going to the compound was far greater than that of frustrated villagers. He'd toyed with the idea of driving to the compound, but every time he thought a reason for heading off, another good reason came for him to stay. Even making the trip to the village of the murdered two men seemed too much effort on this hot day.

One of the men who'd accompanied Jonathon placed his hands on the Chiefs desk.

'We have spoken together today, as a village. We want you to come to our village tonight to talk with us, to tell us what you are going to do. We are fearful of what might happen, what could happen and that we fear for our lives.' Jonathon interrupted his friend.

'Chief Gabir this is something that will effect you, if this militia grows, it will move this way. It will move through our village and others until it gets to you, then you will be forced to do something.'

Chief Gabir didn't like being told what to do and this situation was starting to deeply frustrate him.

'I will not come tonight. I will not be told what to do, I am in charge here. I do hear you and I do hear your concerns. I have other commitments tonight but I will come to your village tomorrow. I will speak to the family and I will speak with...' He looked down at his notes to remind himself of the name... 'Asim. I will speak to them both and find out what I can. But I will tell you that I can't simply go to the compound you are talking about. If it is there, as you say and if there are numbers of soldiers, there is nothing I alone can do. Now please, go back home and I will come to your village tomorrow morning.' The Chief stood up and rudely ushered the men out of his station. As they left, closing the door behind them, Gabir sat back down falling into his chair. This was the last thing he wanted to deal with, but at least he'd managed to put it off until tomorrow. He was looking forward to going home and doing nothing tonight but eat and sleep.

The three men walked out of the building. They hadn't managed to persuade the Chief to go with them but at least they'd put pressure on him to start making some enquiries. Jonathon knew this was going to take some pushing from their part, but with the help of his friends, they might just get the help they needed. They walked back to the village, still feeling the stress from the previous few days, talking little and taking longer than normal to walk the distance back home. This was a situation that had effected everyone in the village, there was no getting away from it.

By the time they'd got back to the village, the sky was almost black. The sun had gone down and there was little light left in the sky. The three men headed back to their homes for the rest of the night. No one wanted to stay out tonight, the mood in the village was very quiet, sombre and divorced from that of the village just four days ago. Jonathon walked through his doorway and was met by his wife.

'How did you get on Jonathon?' Leila, his wife asked.

'That man, Chief Gabir is a fool. He hasn't done anything today but make phantom calls to other police Chief's in the area. He's not going to help us. He says he's coming here tomorrow to talk with Peter's mother and Asim. But I doubt he'll make the effort. I just don't understand the man.'

Jonathon sat down and took a long deep breath. It was a stressful time for him, for his family and for the village. The once strong willed man, the same man who would do anything for anyone, would fight a lion if it meant gaining the respect of his friends, was now a shadow of his previous self. Jonathon's son Damian walked in and greeted his father by giving him a huge hug. Jonathon always hid his feelings from his son. It was so important to him, much like his relationship with his own father, to be seen only as both physically and mentally strong. Jonathon had never once shown his true emotions to his son and for the best part, Damian only saw his father as a strong man who had the respect of his friends and others in the village. He was proud of his father and deeply wanted to be like him when he grew up.

Jonathon suddenly perked up, like nothing had happened during the previous few days. He greeted Damian and they sat for a while, talking about what they'd done in the day. 'Where is your sister Damian?' Jonathon asked. 'She's still out with Asim, they've spent the day together, again! I've not seen her all day.' Jonathon looked at his wife and she smiled in reply. It was a smile of comfort but yet said so much. When Damian went outside, Leila explained to Jonathon that Sabrina had been comforting Asim the entire day. He was trying to put a brave face on the situation but it was clear to all that he was upset at the loss of his friend. 'I told Sabrina that she should be with him today, but I'm expecting her back shortly. Maybe we can eat together Jonathon.' She put an arm over his shoulder and kissed his cheek.

After Sabrina had come back, they all eat dinner together. It was a simple meal of lamb and rice served on plates they'd had for years. The family, like so many in the area weren't wealthy. They didn't have much money and much of what they had they bartered away for supplies as and when they needed it. It was a simple life, but one for which they were completely accustomed to. They rarely went without and had little need for more than what they had. Like many other nights, when they sat and eat dinner together, they enjoyed one another's company and told stories of the day. They were a close family and with the inclusion of Asim, they had one more mouth around the home to tell stories.

'Where is Asim Sabrina?' Jonathon asked.

'He's having dinner with his family tonight father. He might come over later though if that's okay?'

'Yes of course he can, I look forward to seeing him. How's he been today?' Sabrina looked at Damian before answering. She knew they didn't want Damian knowing what had happened, so when she answered, she left out certain parts.

Damian's ears pricked up and his attention was focused elsewhere. 'What's that noise?' He asked. But no one heard anything. There was a dull, very quiet noise emanating from outside, then from no where, Asim rushed through the door.

'There back!' He shouted loudly as he looked at Jonathon. The dull and quiet noise from moments before had already grown louder and was now easily heard by the family. The noise of a few vehicles could be heard, still a distance away, but definitely distinctive to the villagers. Jonathon ran outside and looked out across the fields towards the dusty road. Sure enough there were lights coming from the road, still half a mile away but approaching quickly. He ran back inside and told Sabrina to taker her brother and go with Asim. Jonathon then looked at Asim and told him to run in the other direction and to not stop until they were far enough away from the village.

'What's happening Father?' She asked. 'They've come back and this time they've brought company, there's a few vehicles coming, quickly... go!' We'll do what we can here, but it's dangerous for you.

As the General rounded up his soldiers, he told them to prepare for a small battle. Each of the young men and boys, the youngest of whom were twelve, stood in front of the General with a weapon to their side. He walked up and down in front of them and explained why they would be fighting.

'We are fighting tonight for our country and for our freedom. These people want to take it away from us. They think they can take what is ours and they support the very people we oppose. They came here and murdered our family and tonight we take back our rights.' He spoke with passion and anger in his voice. He believed in what he said and had a profound way of getting his point across. The many children who'd been on the compound believed every word he said. Some had been there for so long, they couldn't remember what it was like to be young and care free. They'd lost what childlike innocence they had and now only saw anger in the faces of their fellow soldiers. They felt proud to fight for the General and felt an immense sense of pride when they held and fired their weapon. They felt like men, they felt like soldiers.

As the children and men got into vehicles, they each sat side by side, not talking, just looking forward. There was no cowardliness in their expressions and few felt anything other than excitement for what they were about to do. For some, this was a first mission and it would proof they could act like men. The General and other senior figures in the compound had spoken with them individually earlier in the day. They'd made it clear what they would be doing, this was about retribution, gaining territory and to gain more soldiers for the forthcoming war. For each person, whether child or teen, they put an arm over their shoulders, gave them a drink and made them feel like a they had to prove something. The main goal with these children was to turn them quickly from adolescence to fighting machine, no looking back and no questions asked.

Each soldier carried a weapon and a few bottles with gasoline and a bit of rag protruding from the top of the bottle. Each of the soldiers had made a few of their own bottles and carried them on their laps in the vehicles. They were ready to wreak havoc and do exactly as instructed.

The four old pickup trucks carrying eight people in each, skidded to a halt in the dusty village. They'd each sped to the village the General had described. Although he didn't know the two boys they'd stopped a few nights back, he knew where they were heading. He'd known the village and the people who lived there from when he was a youngster. In his eyes they were all farmers, all lacked ambition, foresight and vision as to what the Government was doing, they were all cowards and would pay for this. As he jumped out of the vehicle he shouted at the soldiers to get out and go to their own corner of the village. No one was to get out of the area and everyone was to be round up. Those who opposed them were to be shot and any trouble makers were to be taken out before they could sound an alarm or cause problems for them. Their gasoline bottles were to be thrown into buildings to drive people out. They were to damage what they could and destroy what they could. Tonight was all about the havoc they could cause and the rampage was to create complete carnage.

One soldier got out of his vehicle, jumping from the back of the truck. He dropped his bottle on the floor and quickly picked them up, none had been damaged. As he picked them up he saw his first target. He placed the bottle on the floor and took a small match box from his pocket. He struck a match, watching the small stick light up in the darkness of the night. He placed the matchstick over one of the bottle and waited for the small rag to light up. As the flames slowly increased, he watched the bottle, then as the flame grew he looked at his target and threw the bottle with all his might. The bottle flew straight through a window and shattered. There was a small explosion from within the house and the soldier watched as the flames engulfed the inside of the building. He heard screams from inside the house and people fled out of their home. As they did, the soldier was outside ready for them to come out. The first was a young girl, followed by her mother and lastly the father. As they ran out of their home, the soldier was startled by the speed of which they got out, running directly into his path. The moment he'd thrown the handmade grenade, he'd held his gun aloft and aimed it towards the front door. The moment the family came out, they didn't stand a chance against the young soldier. It was the first mission he'd been on and he was completely unaware of what to expect. His gun fired bullets, splattering the front of the home and with it, the family lay on the ground. The young soldier was aware of what he'd done, but his expression was blank.

Those were the first shots fired that night, however they weren't the last. People were shot at and harassed into areas around the village. Buildings were destroyed and some were on fire. With no one to put out the flames, the fires grew and peoples homes were being destroyed. Their possessions lost forever and their lives completely turned upside down.

Few people were rounded up. The mission was exactly as the General had expected. He knew the young soldiers would be overwhelmed. In the darkness, with flames everywhere and with shouting and screaming all around them, they would be more at ease firing their weapons, than doing as originally instructed. He knew they would be scarred by this mission, but he would be there for them. He and the other senior leaders would ensure that any negatives, any emotions the boys showed would be pushed aside. This would stand as a great experience for them and would be used well during future conflicts.

As the tall flames licked the area and the last gun shots were fired, villagers were scattered around, not knowing where to go or what to do. The noise of the fire as it destroyed buildings was loud and could be heard over everything. Windows were smashing and the echo of gunfire could still be heard. As the carnage halted, a man could be heard shouting over the noise of the still screaming villagers and flames. Few people heard what he was saying. His words fell silent over the majority of people who were suffering from shock and disbelief at what had occurred. The soldiers got into their vehicles and sped off down the dusty road and into the darkness. For all the shots fired and carnage created, only three young men were taken, three more to fight for the General.

As the last of the four vehicles drove out of sight, the villagers were left to beat out the flames and gather what they could before the fires would eventually take their belongings.

Jonathon and Lella's home had been completely destroyed. They were some of the lucky ones who after leaving their home had done as instructed. Their home had been destroyed by a soldier who seamed to know what he was doing and didn't fire his weapon on a whim. They, along with a few other people had been shoved to the ground in the middle of the dusty road. As people all around them were being harassed, they could do nothing but watch in disbelief as people were being fired at from all around them and homes were being destroyed.

As the last of the vehicles had gone, Jonathon had run into the home and gathered what he could before the flames overwhelmed him. He left the home with just a few things and passed a few to his wife. He then grabbed her arm and they ran into the wilderness towards where they'd sent their children. Tears were falling from their eyes, their hearts were beating faster than ever before in their lives and they'd lost all feeling of pain in their feet as they ran over rocks, tripped over sticks and fell to the floor as they misjudged where what they were running over. It was of no importance to them. 'Sabrina, Damian, Asim!' They shouted as they ran in the direction for which they'd sent the children running no more than twenty or so minutes ago. They hoped with all their hearts the children would hear them, that they were all still alive. But they could see nothing in the darkness and the further away from the village they got, the quieter the screams and sounds of destruction were. They both stopped running with exhaustion and both looked either side, still shouting the names of the children.

'They may have gotten far Leila, please God say they got away.' Jonathon said whilst looking out into the darkness.

Leila was crying and was shouting for the children to return. She was beginning to lose faith, falling to her knees she began to wale. From the shadows, three figures could just be made out, walking slowly towards them. Jonathon was the first to spot them and pulled at his wife when he realised who it was. Asim had managed to get the three of them to safety, well out of the way of the soldiers and lights from their vehicles. As they neared, both Jonathon and Leila ran towards them. The embrace was the longest they'd ever given their children. The three children were unaware of the carnage the village was in, that would follow as they walked back. Jonathon and Leila were still crying, though Jonathon was wiping his tears away, trying to stay focused. However every time he looked up at his son and daughter, his eyes welled up and he pulled them in, hugging them tightly, not wanting to let go.

It would be the first time their family was ever put in such danger.

Chief Gabir had a typical morning. Nothing eventful had happened and nothing noteworthy had landed on his old wooden desk. He had nothing better to do, so decided to make his way to see this "Asim" and the lady who'd lost her father and son a few days back. At some point he'd have to make the effort, but where this would lead he had no idea. But he was certain of something, there was no way he was going the extra mile to take a trip to the village where this supposed "compound" was. It wasn't worth his time and he wasn't about to put his life in danger by getting involved in anything too big and out of his control.

Reluctantly and out of duty, he'd gotten into his Toyota 4x4 and driven to the village. Although the fires had been put out, there was still smoke in the air. As Gadir got closer, the first thing he noticed was the smell of smoke. Then pulling up and getting out of his vehicle he saw the devastation left behind from the night before. Dead bodies had been lined up with sheets over them. People had makeshift bandages over blooded wounds and the devastation was now all too real. The expression on Gadir's face said it all. He'd never seen anything like this before, he'd never seen a murdered corpse and never had to deal with a father of a murdered family. This was all too overwhelming and in an instant a cold sweat and a heavy mind numbing feeling fell upon him. As men and women grabbed at his shirt for his attention, all he could do was stand in a deafened silence. He was staring blankly at the charred remains of a home and a crying mother standing in the doorway of what remained of her old life.

# CHAPTER 13
### (Present day)

After the family had got off the transport at the port town in Egypt and when he was alone, Jonathon unzipped his coat pocket and pulled out his money. The amount he paid for transit to the port town was expensive and more than he wanted to pay. However the journey had saved them weeks, if not months of walking. After the siege on their village and after the deaths of multiple families, including that of the death of Asim's mother and father. they felt they had no choice but to abandon their old lives. The lack of respect from the local authorities and because there was now an increased risk from the militia, the few families who remained felt they had nowhere to go other than leaving their country of origin. Leila's sister, who had travelled to Europe years before, had sent a few letters back home and made her new way of life in Italy sound both intriguing and desirable. On many occasions Leila and Jonathon had talked about the possibility of moving away from their home. However it was always Leila who instigated conversations and wanted to move at some point during her life, to be closer again with her sister. Jonathon on the other hand wanted to stay. He always argued there were plenty of good opportunities at home, that life wasn't always better in Europe and that she should be careful of what she hoped for. But after the aftermath of the militia attack on their village and the murder of Jonathon's close friends, he felt downtrodden and exhausted of hope of a positive future. Leila had made the decision to leave for Europe and Jonathon had followed… as well as a few other families who felt the same. The families had gathered what they could and any money they could rustle up, then fled. For all concerned it had been a difficult decision but a necessary one. Staying at home had bad memories, their village was full of ghosts and hope was all but lost. As far as they were concerned, Europe had everything.

The money Jonathon had paid for the faster transit to the port town in Egypt had left them little in the way of funds for crossing the sea. Jonathon knew money would be tight and if they had to spend a long time awaiting the transport to Europe, both he and Asim might have to find some work to pay for the additional time spent in North Africa. He conceded it was just something they may have to do. Jonathon counted the money in his hands and placed it carefully back in his pocket, zipping it up after.

The old ransacked coach, which carried them the remainder of the journey, was built in the nineteen eighties. It was ghastly both inside and out. Rusting, with broken windows and missing panels and judging by the number of times it had broken down, the engine had clearly seen better days. But despite the consistency of the many engine failures, it had gotten them to the port town and a camp surrounded by a tall metal fence. Although they hadn't seen the Mediterranean sea, they could smell it in the air. However being no one in the group had seen the sea before, it was only a change in the odour which gave away their location. That damp, salty fresh air you smell when close to any coastline.

The camp site was heaving with people and none in the group had any idea of where to go. A man, who looked like he was some kind of a security guard at the front of the site, approached Jonathon and asked him why he'd come. The guard was used to random people turning up, it was a regular daily occurrence.

Recruited months back, the guard's feelings towards these people descending on his country, causing mischief and mayhem had been a huge frustration to him. He had no sympathy towards them nor any regards towards their wellbeing. This was a job and it paid for food on his table. But after a month of looking at the same downtrodden, exhausted faces of families crossing the line into the camp, he realised what this place was. It was a sanctuary, a place of transit and safety from whatever it was these people were fleeing. Yes, there was crime in the camp, these people were desperate, some starving, sick and some just lost souls. But being that people still came and remained here, it was obvious they were better off inside than out. Without noticing his change in opinion, his face turned from that of frustration and anger to that of humbleness, humility and friendship. He was the first person many of these people would see when they arrived at the camp and he wanted to make the first thing they saw to be something warm and friendly.

Greeting Jonathon with a friendly smile and pat on his shoulder, the guard told Jonathon where he was, where he should go and who he should see. The man he had to see was called Ahmed and was down at the bottom of the site. Jonathon asked Asim to look after the family whilst he went searching for the site administrator. Leila, Sabrina, Asim and Damian all sat down with the few belongings they'd brought.

As he walked through he couldn't help but see many people just sitting around. Men and women sat talking to one another whilst children played in the dirt, kicking cans around or running aimlessly as children do. He couldn't help but think this wasn't the place they had hoped for. Spending time here would be like wasting your life away and despite all that had happened, he wasn't ready to change the habit of a lifetime and not be productive.

After ten minutes of walking past hundreds of makeshift tents and what he guessed was a thousand people, Jonathon eventually got to the bottom of the site. Past a mile of wasteland, he saw the blue of the Mediterranean sea. It was still far off, however it was there in the distance, unattainable through the eight foot tall metal fence, but there nonetheless. He'd never seen the sea before. Jonathon had spent his entire life in a landlocked country and there was simply no reason to venture off elsewhere. He'd seen a lake before, years ago in his youth, but the sea was something altogether different. To Jonathon, it was the gateway to a new life, perhaps the start of something amazing and for the first time in a long time, he felt that feeling of hope again. He removed himself from the fence and walked around asking for Ahmed. Many people in the site were from different countries, it was obvious to Jonathon by not only the colour of their skin but the multiple languages people were speaking. It was as if he were on another planet and in an instance, that brief feeling of hope was replaced by a feeling of being lonely and lost. He felt overwhelmed and completely alien to this place. He was missing his home and couldn't wait to get back to the top of the site again and find his family. However he first had to find this Ahmed and make arrangements for their safe transit to Italy. That was priority, to get out of this lost place and back into a normal way of life… if there would ever be such a thing.

Continuing to ask people for the man called Ahmed, Jonathon was finally offered something in the way of success when a couple of men pointed in the direction of a tent situated in the corner of the site.

As Jonathon approached and tried to walk in, two large men walked out and stopped him before he entered.

'Who are you?' They aggressively asked.

Jonathon was taken aback for a second, not so much by the size of the two men, but because they spoke his language. 'My name is Jonathon, my family and I have travelled far and arrived here today. They're at the top of the site with friends of ours. I just wanted to know what we need to do, where to go and how we get across that.' He said whilst pointing at the sea in the background.

One of the men stepped inside the large white

tent and momentarily walked back out. He told Jonathon to go inside. As Jonathon entered, he was surprised by the cleanliness and organised structure to the tent. There were desks, a computer, chairs and what looked like a bed in the corner, surrounded by curtains. He thought that perhaps this person lived and worked here.

'Hello, my name is Ahmed, I'm the administrator here. Take a seat over there and we'll get you processed.'

After a few minutes, Ahmed sat down at the desk and took a few papers from a drawer. He started taking some notes from Jonathon, then told him where there was a free tent. It had only become unoccupied today but would house both his family and the others who had taken the trip with him.

'That would be almost thirty people in one tent!' Jonathon said whilst looking shocked.

'Do you know how many people are here at this site Jonathon?' Ahmed asked. 'There are currently just over two thousand people here, sharing a mixture of large and small tents. If you want to get to Europe, you need to understand that the next few months are going to be difficult.'

Ahmed stood up and walked round to Jonathon, standing in front of him.

'Listen, this is the worst place on Earth. It's filthy, there is little in the way of toilets and showers. People, such as your family will struggle to find food, work and sometimes even safety. It's the price you pay for coming here to my country on your way to Europe.' He patted Jonathon on the shoulder. 'But with my help Jonathon, you will eventually get out of here and get your wish.'

He went on to add that crossings would be periodical, there was no real timeline or long planned crossings. You got an idea of when you were leaving, at best a three day window and you would need to pay whoever got you to the boat. It was as simple as that.

'I do not arrange any crossings here, nor do I take any money from you. We, that is my country, expect you to make illegal attempts to cross and it is my job to discourage you and look after you whilst you're here. If you make an attempt you could be stopped or you could get across to Europe. If you are stopped, you will have lost your money and… more than likely be brought back here. Now… which country do you want to get to?'

After Ahmed had asked to see the other families who'd travelled with Jonathon, one of the large men at the entrance of Ahmed's tent, escorted Jonathon back to the top of the site. From there, he took the families to what would be their tent for the next few months. When they arrived, the man told them to wait outside for a short while. He walked in alone and kicked out the family who'd taken up residency. It was a careless act of violence, more shoving and reckless pushing than fists, however an act of violence nonetheless and certainly something none of the awaiting tenants were expecting.

After the family had been pushed out and their few belongings had been thrown outside, the man stuck his head through the tent and told them to come in.

'Get yourself settled in your own area of the tent, I'll be back in a second to go over some site rules that I need to tell you.' The man then walked back outside and dealt with the family who'd taken it upon themselves to use the tent. He beat the man and kicked him as he grabbed at his few belongings whilst trying to walk away, his family in tow. They walked off and before long were camouflaged by the other people in the site. The man then walked back to the tent and stood at the entrance. He pulled a crumpled piece of paper from his pocket and started to read the site rules.

'There is no thieving of anything from anyone else in this site. Fighting or violence of any kind is not acceptable. Moving to another tent is forbidden without consent of the site administrator.'

He went on listing the rules of the site and added that failure to comply with the rules would result in being evicted from the camp site indefinitely. Adding the people who were in this tent would be dealt with harshly if they repeated their offence. 'They were just lucky I'm busy sorting you out and... because I'm in a good mood! My name's Omar.' He looked Jonathon up and down, like he was examining him, then said; 'let me know if you have any concerns or if you need anything.' He said goodbye and left the tent, leaving the families to themselves. Jonathon looked at Leila and smiled. 'So we're here now, Italy next!' He then looked at his friends and told them to make their way to the corner tent and ask for Ahmed. Telling them to refer to him when they gave their details across.

The next few days came and went without much happening. Despite the cramped conditions and the lack of privacy, the families were more content with the fact they were in one place and not constantly moving. It was the first time in a month they were still for more than one day. Jonathon had managed to walk around the site and get an idea of how things ran. He also made enquiries about how much the crossing would cost and roughly when they would expect news of a crossing for themselves. The amount of people wanting to cross was huge and there were only so many crossings each week. To make it more difficult for the coastguards, there was no routine to the crossings. But from the sounds of things, it seemed clear to Jonathon the authorities practically allowed you to cross. The chance of getting on a boat and evading the local authorities was likely. But there was also the perilous risk of crossing the Mediterranean However any risk was downplayed.

The family still had a small amount of food, but that was running out and soon, Jonathon was going to have to venture out of the camp to find some local shops. Whilst walking around the site, Jonathon had made a few contacts, people who were housed a few tents down from them, though neither had families and only looked after themselves. From sitting down with his family, he got up and walked to find the three men he'd chatted to earlier in the day. He hoped they would be able to take him into the local town. Jonathon's confidence was still down. Normally he'd have ventured off himself, however he just didn't feel up to it alone. He was also concerned about being robbed or attacked. There had been stories of people venturing off the site and being attacked by local thugs taking vengeance for the land they occupied and for the jobs they'd taken. Since coming to the site, Jonathon had taken it upon himself to make new contacts, rather than keeping himself to himself and sticking with the villagers who'd travelled with them. Although they acted friendly within the confides of the tent, outside it was vitally important to ensure they had the upper hand. There was going to be only a few people who could cross at a time and they had to be first. Jonathon would look to take advantage of any possibility he could. However the one thing he wouldn't do was screw over his old friends, it was not in him to do such a thing.

Jonathon walked up to the tent his three new contacts occupied. It was a single tent and was one of the smallest in the site. It was so small and tatty looking that he wondered if it would even be rain proof if there were a down-poor. He walked up to the tent and heard voices inside.

'Hello!' Jonathon asked before the tent was unzipped from the inside. Three men were sat in their own privacy playing a card game. He felt awkward asking the question, not wanting to sound like he was desperate for their company and the safety of walking as a group, but it was something he was going to have to do.

'I'm walking into town for the first time, I know it's an ask, but would you men mind accompanying me. After hearing some of those stories about people being attacked, I thought it would be safer going in with you strong men.'

'Yes of course, let us finish this game, there's

money on this one.' One of the men said, smiling at Jonathon and his friends as he placed his cards face up on the floor.

The three men had been at the site for over half a year and made their first attempt at crossing two months back. However they'd lost everything when their boat was stopped by the authorities and were brought back to the site. Because they'd caused no problems, nor been mixed in any in trouble since their first day, the site Administrator had taken pity on them and given them refuge once again. However it was little help to them, other than giving them a "roof" over their heads. Now with nothing but the shirts on their backs and a small collection of money, they were working to get the funds together to make another attempt at crossing. But that would be next year. The cost of crossing was over a thousand dollars and obtaining that amount of cash was going to require a lot of working. They would be stuck here for the foreseeable future. But for all their bad luck, their spirits were high, or at least as high as the situation would allow for.

As they were leaving the site Asim ran up to Jonathon and asked if he could come along. The three men hadn't met Asim up until this point and Jonathon introduced him as his son in law. They shook hands and all walked into town.

The walk into town was thirty minutes and it

gave Jonathon time to get to know the three men a little more. The road was long and straight and as they walked, cars sped past, occasionally beeping their horns at the five men walking.

'Why do they beep?' Asked Jonathon.

'Either to let us know we're walking on a highway or because they don't like us loitering in their country. I wouldn't normally mind, but since we were stopped by them whilst trying to leave their country, it now gets to me. It's just typical isn't it? But one thing we've come to learn, since being stopped on the boat is the authorities purposely allow a certain number of boats to cross. We were just unlucky.'

'No!... Seriously? What do you mean?' Asked Jonathon.

'It's true, they allow around sixty percent of the boats to cross, whilst stopping the rest. They don't want us in their country any more than we want to stay. Imagine they stopped us all, their country would be overrun with people wanting to make the journey. No, they let a good number of the boats cross, they turn a blind eye. But of course they have to stop a number of the boats and show Europe they're doing what they can. And I'm pretty sure the site Administrator Ahmed, tells the authorities what's happening, when crossings are occurring and who's on the boats. The man comes across all helpful and understanding, but he's being paid a fortune to keep the authorities up to date with information, believe me!'

'So the whole thing is a game of luck, how do you trust that you'll ever get out of here?'

'Well we put our trust in our hard work and Allah of course! But that's not all. Next time we'll pay more and it'll ensure we get across. You see, there are ways and means of escaping this country that don't include going through Ahmed to arrange your lottery voyage. If I were you Jonathon, I would pay the extra money and ensure you get across. With your family as well, you can't afford to get caught and start all over again.' He looked at his friends walking ahead of them. 'We can, we only have ourselves to look after, but you have a family wanting to get across to Europe.'

'Well how much are we talking about then?' Jonathon asked.

'It's not cheap, one of the men who work for Ahmed help run the crossings.'

'Omar?' Jonathon Asked.

'Yes that's right, you've met him then?'

'Yes, briefly. He helped us settle into our tent

and in the process kicked another family out, beating the husband all the way. But other than that he seems a nice man.'

'Nice? I'm not sure about that. But if you get on the right side of him, he can be a useful contact. He runs the operation from here, doing it behind the back of Ahmed. He charges two thousand to get across, per person. He doesn't offer crossings to people he doesn't get to know, or people that he doesn't like. He seems to enjoy watching people suffer in the camps. Have you heard the screams in the middle of the night?'

'Maybe, yes. But I assumed they were just people having nightmares or getting into stupid fights. Why?'

'That's usually from Omar and his thugs. It comes to those who fail to pay their fee for crossing on time or if you tell someone you're going and people start asking questions. If it gets back to Omar, he'll take his frustrations out on you. I've also heard he's been known to kidnap people and hold them hostage for money. He isn't the sort of person who you want to annoy. But if you're decent, you pay him what's agreed, you keep your head down and do as you're told, then you'll be okay.'

'It sounds like I'll wait for Ahmed's way out then, I just hope it comes sooner rather than later. I don't fancy making my family stay around here for any longer than they have to.' Jonathon said.

After arriving into the town and taking a walk around, Asim and Jonathon went into the market and purchased a few items of food to take back to the camp with them. At present, money wasn't a huge issue for Jonathon, he'd managed to save an amount over the years and had sold almost everything he owned before leaving the village. It was enough for them to get to Egypt and just about enough for a crossing, however if they had to stay here much longer, he would need to find a local job. But to pay Omar two thousand per person was simply out of the question, regardless of it being a more guaranteed crossing.

Before walking back, Asim had decided he would stay behind in the town and walk back later. It was fairly quiet and not many people were about, so Asim felt like he would be safe staying on his own. The youngest man out of the three, offered to stay with Asim, as long as he brought him a drink later. Asim agreed and the two young men walked off together.

Jonathon walked back with the two other men, along the road and back to the site. When he got back, he thanked his two new friends and gave them a few coins for their time. It was money he would possibly need later, but for now it seemed as important to make good friends. The two men took the money and thanked Jonathon. They shook his hand. 'Thank you Jonathon, you're a good man and I hope you get across to Europe soon.' As they walked off, Jonathon watched them as they crawled into their small tent. He felt sorry for the men, alone, no families and only a small tent to live in. It was a difficult way of life for so many people, he only hoped Europe would be worth the sacrifice.

# CHAPTER 14

Picking up a bat from the side and walking out of the entrance, Omar was greeted by two other men. As they made their way to the camp site, Omar explained who it was they were sorting out that night and what they'd done to anger him.

Pulling up at the front of the site, Omar was approached by the guard. It was a different guard to that of the man who'd welcomed in Jonathon and his friends. This guard wasn't quite as friendly, he'd been hired to deal with people at night. Such people walking around after darkness were usually trouble and the person at the entrance of the site would need to be tougher and prepared to deal with certain difficulties.

'Omar!' The guard said whilst extending his hand to greet him.

'It's good to see you again Amir'.

As he pulled his hand away, the guard placed the money Omar had given him in his pocket. It wasn't a huge amount of cash, but on the side, it was enough to keep him quiet in the event he heard a skirmish later on. There were other guards periodically walking around, but at this time they would be around the other side of the site and wouldn't hear what was about to happen. But in the event they did, Omar would also give them something for their troubles.

Omar told Amir where they were heading and got back into the vehicle. As the truck slowly crept past Amir, he caught sight of the two other men with Omar. They looked straight ahead, giving him no eye contact whatsoever. They looked mean, like they wouldn't think twice about clubbing you to death. Their eyes were focused directly in front of them like they were only interested in what they were about to do.

The truck pulled up to the medium sized tent and all three men got out, flashlights in hand and quickly and uninvited, walked straight into the tent. As one man went to stand, one of the thugs with Omar kneed him to the ground, pushing him back to the floor even before he could get to his knees. The man knew who these men where and he didn't bother to try and stand again. He sat on the floor and watched as they walked over to the far corner of the tent.

Even before the man they were after had fully

woken, the two men had grabbed him by the arms and were dragging him to his feet. Omar stepped up and smashed his bat into the back of the man's leg, rendering his stance useless and forcing him to collapsed. Holding him aloft and taking his weight, the two men either side of him turning him to face Omar.

Now the entire tent was awake and could see the flashlights in the corner of the tent. It was obvious what was happening, but no one wanted to get involved. Whatever the man had done to anger Omar was his business. Everyone knew not to mess with him, you reaped what you sewed. However his family were a lot more concerned. Grasping at the leg of Omar, pleading for the man's life. But it was no good. As the man attempted to talk, Omar thumped him in the stomach with his bat. Winded, the man winced in pain as his head dropped. Despite his arms both being held, he tried to clutch at his stomach as the feeling of sickness fell upon him.

Omar lifted his bat and looked as if he were about to hit the mans wife, but before he did, he stopped as she held up her hands in defence. He pointed at her and then held up his finger against his lips to signal for her to stop talking. He turned to the men and motioned for them to escort the man to the truck. They walked out of the tent and pushed the man in the back. Then getting in themselves, they drove away from the site, past the guard and straight out onto the highway back to Omar's home.

As they drove down the road, the kidnapped man tried talking, but before he could get a word out, one of Omar's men again punched the man in the stomach and told him to keep quiet. The man knew what he'd done and thought to himself that surely it didn't warrant losing his life over… Or had it? He questioned himself again, but this time he answered his own question with the most negative of responses. Yes, it was possible that he'd angered the worst man he could have and potentially he'd never see his family again. A tear rolled down his cheek, but he didn't whimper nor try and plead. He sat there in silence thinking of any excuse he could.

Pulling up at Omar's home, the truck stopped and all personnel got out of the vehicle and walked up to the door. Omar unlocked the door and the four men walked in. Walking into a dark empty room, the two men pushed the kidnapped man to the floor. Omar only had one small dull bulb which hung from the ceiling on a cable. It wasn't bright, but managed to light up the centre of the room and a portion of the walls.

The man was on his knees in the centre, looking up at Omar, his hands aloft, begging for forgiveness.

'I didn't mean to offend you Omar, truly I didn't.'

He said looking up at his captor.

'I told you not to tell anyone what was happening. So how did I find out from another party that you couldn't make payment for your crossing?'

The man tried to talk, but was immediately put down by Omar, cutting him off before he could finish his sentence.

'Don't interrupt me when I'm talking, you've talked too much and now it's my turn. Do you know what happens if people find out what I'm doing here?' It was a rhetorical question and he motioned for the man to hold his silence. 'If the site administrator finds out what I'm doing, I'll be sent to jail, possibly worse. I'm doing a service here, not only for you people but to my country. The more people I can get across the sea to Europe the less people there are here in Egypt. If this stops, then not only will it get more crowded at the site, but crime goes up, there's more violence, more sickness and death. This place needs assistance, it needs order, and I'm the man to do it. It's people like you who bring chaos to my order. Talking to anyone who'll lend an ear. Blabbing to just about anyone who cares to listen. I told you not to talk and I told you to only accept my offer of transit if you could afford it. I've numbers to fill on the boat. Your boat leaves in three days and I'm only hearing now that you don't have the funds. I have numbers to fill, I have a boss and likewise he has a boss. Everyone has a fucking boss and everyone needs to get paid. Do you want me to look stupid in front of my boss?' He angrily asked the man on his knees.

'No Omar, I'm sorry. I, I... the money just ran out, I thought I could gather more but it just wasn't enough time.'

'Well that's too bad, you've forced my hand.'

Jude wasn't the liveliest of children. Being that he had no other brothers to run around with, he'd got used to playing on his own and making his own fun. On a few occasions his parents had caught him talking to himself. Not to an imaginary friend, but just to himself, like he was having his own conversation. Over the years and when at home, he'd got used to playing alone and it had also taught him to keep his thoughts and feelings bottled up. In some respects he felt like an only child and with it, came a certain responsibility, a natural ability to hide his true feelings. Perhaps that side of him was natural, or perhaps a side which his parents hadn't helped with. But nonetheless, it was there.

It had been the previous year when Jude had been watching the news. His mother had left the living room and left Jude watching his favourite recorded program. When that had finished, the news automatically turned on. The news reader, before showing the report, mentioned that some images were graphical and upsetting. The report was on the immigration of African's to Europe. The illegal crossings which happen almost daily from Northern Africa and the difficult and sometimes treacherous journeys which people were making. Images of people laying on their front, bobbing in the water, drowned whilst making their attempts to cross. One image was that of a small child laying washed up on a beach in Italy. His small body laying still, face down on the beach. His family having given their lives for the opportunity to get to Europe. It was this image which had stuck with Jude and not once had he mentioned it to anyone. He kept it bottled up, locked up and away deep in his psyche. Seeing the many passengers on the small boat, some wearing life jackets, others not. There were images of people in the water and images of dead bodies. It was enough to grab the attention of the small boy and to scar him for life. It was this one moment which had given him his fear of the water and it remained with him the entire time they were onboard of the vessel, drifting in the middle of the Mediterranean sea. He'd kept his thoughts and the image of the drowned child hidden away. Occasionally he'd forgotten about it, mostly when he was having fun with his sister or father. But on the odd occasion when he was alone and he looked out to sea, he remembered. The image of the small

African child, laying face down, soaked to the bone and dead on the beach having given his life for the "ultimate prize".

As the first of many punches and kicks were thrown at the man on his knees, he fell to the floor. At first he was able to raise his arms to shield his face from the many blows. However after what seamed an eternity, each blow was camouflaged by an overwhelming pain that went through his body. Before long he lay unconscious on the floor, blood pouring from his wounds.

'Is he dead?' Asked Omar to one of his thugs.

'No he isn't boss, do you want him dead?'

'No, leave him, he's had enough.' Omar said, whilst holding his hand aloft, motioning for the beating to stop. Omar walked over to the man, still laying still on the floor. He knelt down and slapped the man awake. He coughed and spluttered out some words, which Omar had no understanding of. The man was attempting to plead again. Omar leant close to the man and whispered in his ear.

'This was a warning, do not anger me again. Don't speak of this and do not expect to get across to Europe any time soon. My offer is retracted.' Omar looked up at his two thugs.

'He's done for the night, stand him up and bring

him to the truck. We'll drop him back to the camp site.'

As they drove back to the site, one of Omar's thugs handed the man a dirty towel and told him to wipe himself. He was a little more lucid now and in complete understanding of what he'd done wrong, who he'd wronged and what he had coming to him. He deeply regretted taking Omar up on his offer to get him and his small family to Europe quicker than the normal means. Sitting in the back of the vehicle, knowing he could potentially spend the remainder of his life at the site, he almost wished he'd been killed that night.

On dropping the man back at his tent, Omar's thug pushed the man inside. On seeing her husband land almost at her feet and seeing the condition he'd been left in. She screamed and fell to her knees.Whilst crying for her husband she hugged him and praised her God for bringing him back to her.

On driving back to his home, Omar looked at the driver. 'I'll have to find another three people then. I need to fill that boat. Find me another three people tomorrow, we'll have two days to fill the spaces.

Jonathon woke quickly. The screams of a

woman not ten tents away had awoken him from a deep sleep. He sat bolt upright and noticed as the bright yellow lights from a vehicle drove past his tent. He dared not think about what kind of atrocity had occurred. Laying back down, he carefully placed an arm around his wife and closed his eyes.

# CHAPTER 15

Asim, together with Sabrina and his new friend walked back into town. Asim wanted to show Sabrina there was more to Egypt than solely that of a dirty coach. One week previous on arriving at the site, neither Sabrina nor her mother had ventured out further than a few tents away. On the few occasions they lost sight of their tent, it had always been with Jonathon or Asim, there was no way that neither of the men would allow them to walk out of the tent and around the site alone. It just wasn't the sort of place you felt safe. Whether screams of women in the night or small scuffles during the day, it was clear the site was not a safe place. People were desperate, starving... and lost. Some had been there weeks, months and Jonathon assumed years in the most extreme of situations. It was just an unsafe place to live and he wanted out. Other than his first glimpse of the Mediterranean Sea when he'd first arrived, had he felt good and like he was heading to Europe to start afresh. However one thing after another reminded him this was no place to stay. He would do what he could to keep his family safe until the time came when they could make the trip to Italy and to Leila's sister.

On leaving the camp site and walking to the local town, Asim had warned Sabrina about how the locals felt about outsiders, about the people that simply wanted to leave the country. He made it clear to her that they could find themselves in trouble and that she should keep herself to herself, not look people in the eye and to always stick to main roads. That they would not venture off down back streets or into areas which might be secluded and pose a possible threat. After the death of his friend Peter, Asim's responsibility was to Sabrina and her family, which he now regarded as his own. Jonathon had always welcomed Asim into the family circle. But after the death of Asim's parents and since he kept both Sabrina and Damian out of harms way on that frightful night, Jonathon had regarded Asim as his own son and he had every confidence in him. He knew with every part of his body, that Asim would be true to his name... He would act as her protector and be a part of her life as long as he should live. So when Asim asked to take her into town, he had no doubt she would be safe.

The first thing they did, on walking into town, was to walk through the centre and towards the port. Sabrina and Asim had seen the sea as it edged closer as they walked into town, but now that it lay out in front of them, filling the entire horizon, it was like nothing else they'd seen before. Both stood in awe at the sight that lay in front of them. Both holding hands, they looked out. Never before had they seen anything like it. The sight of turquoise waves overlapping one another and the cool sea breeze blowing through her hair was something new and so refreshing that for a moment Sabrina had forgotten where she was. She turned to Asim and kissed him on the lips.

'Thank you Asim for getting us here. Everything we've been through, but more so yourself. After losing your parents and your home, for all the walking and the blistering heat, you've never once let me down, even at your darkest hour. For that my love I am yours forever.' Never before had she spoken so much from the heart. The emotions of being somewhere alien to her, somewhere which as she spoke, made her feel like she were in Heaven, made her more emotional than ever before. She kissed him once again and sat down.

'It's quite something, isn't it Asim?' His new friend said, whilst also sitting on the floor staring at the sea. 'I've been here now for close to six months, this place feels more like home by the day. There's times when I think I'll just stay here and live in Egypt. There's far worse places to be and despite the concerns for our safety and the money situation, I sometimes think it would be the easiest thing to do. I mean what's in Europe anyway? It's not the promised land that people say it is. No where is, there'll still be trouble, discrimination and poverty. It's not like you get across and all of a sudden your troubles just disappear. It's different for your family I guess, you've people on the other side, a destination. We're just heading across in the hope of finding a better life than what we've left behind. There's no guarantees.'

His words felt uneasy to Asim and Sabrina who was listening intently to what the young man was saying. It was true, there were no guarantees and as much as they all wished things would be brighter in Europe, it just wasn't as easy as that. Sabrina couldn't help but wonder whether making the perilous journey would be worth the risk.

'I hear what you're saying.' Asim said. And you're right, there's no guarantees, but we've come so far already, we couldn't just give up now.'

'That money in your pocket Asim, have you noticed how it's burning a hole in your pocket already. It won't last. You have to get across before it's too late. Many people don't and they find themselves stuck here in Limbo. They know where the "ultimate prize" is, but it's so unobtainable and so far out of reach. Trust me Asim, make your decision quickly before it's a decision that can't be reversed. That money won't last forever and if you don't find work to pay for your food and crossing... well lets just say, like me, your options will be reduced rapidly.'

Asim stood up and looked at his new friend. He thanked him for his honesty and looked him in the eyes. He grabbed his hand and held it close to his chest. 'Never lose faith my friend, never lose faith in yourself and your life. You make your own luck in life. Come on, let's walk around the town before we head back.

Walking back through town they strolled down one of the main market streets. People were everywhere, walking between stools, searching through boxes of various things to buy, exchanging money for produce and it made Asim feel almost like he belonged. It was a nice feeling and one which he hadn't felt in such a long time. The various smells from the market and the sound of cooking meat filled the air and before long they found themselves standing in front of a stool selling food. They all looked at the food in awe, their mouths dripping and their eyes wide as they watched the food sizzling away.

'Come on you two, my treat.' He handed the trader some money and handed the cooked food to Sabrina and his friend. They took their food off to the side where they sat and devoured the small meal in a matter of minutes. It had been the first proper meal that both Sabrina and Asim had in weeks. They weren't by any means starving, but the constant rations had started to wear thin on their appetites. And now they ate something warm, greasy and fatty, did that long felt hunger disappear. Taking a moment to eat every crumb, they sat and relaxed, again, fully taking in the moment as if it were just a normal day.

They stood up and started to walk back out of town. On reaching the edge of the market, Asim's attention was grabbed. He could see what looked like old wooden stilts holding up a building. It was a makeshift scaffold tower creeping up the outside of a building being refurbished. Asim hadn't seen such a huge tower before and thought it was crazy. 'You'd never catch me up one of those towers.' He said to Sabrina. But as his gaze moved on from the tower, he heard some commotion coming from the top. As he looked up, one or two items fell and landed on the floor with a huge bang. Then came a scream from a man at the top. The scaffold tower was on the verge of collapsing and the three young adults stood watching as the tower leant away from the building, looking like it would collapse at any moment.

The man at the top shouted for help but no one was around other than the three young adults, still with full stomachs. Asim, never one to run from danger, ran towards the scaffold. Not thinking about what could happen if it collapsed upon him, he ran to the bottom. The man at the top was still shouting, but now had taken it upon himself to try and grab onto something to save himself, to save the tower.

Asim could see the man was in trouble, but there was no way he could help. He couldn't push the tower back towards the building, it was far too heavy and the man at the top seamed completely unable to do anything from up there other than shout. In the moments that followed, Asim noticed that a harness midway up the tower had come loose and before he could think of anything else, he was already making his ascent up the ladder. It was obvious this was partly to blame for the towers imminent collapse. The man at the top was holding onto the side with all his might. Fighting against every one of his bodies natural instincts to let go with the force of the towers weight pulling against every one of the fibres in his body.

Asim's friend told Sabrina to stay back and he also got in on the action, trying desperately to push the tower back towards the wall it had been leaning against. It did little, however he called out for more help and shouted at Asim to hurry up. Asim was now only meters away from the strap. It wasn't much, but it was something which had come loose, but had obviously served a purpose. He grabbed the strap from the floor and swung it around the pole it had been previously attached to. As it draped around the pole, Asim pulled it tight, using every one of his muscles to do so. He cried out in pain and frustration as he pulled it tight. Then using the hook, he threw it around the other side of the strap and locked it into position. The scaffold was again tight to the wall.

Asim quickly climbed down and moved away from the tower, still watching in disbelief as it once again leant tight against the wall. The once shouting man at the top was already most of the way down and as he got the ground he ran to Asim and hugged him. He didn't know this young man who'd inadvertently saved him, nor did he know the two other people standing beside him. However he did know what he'd done and was more grateful than ever before in his life.

'Thank you my friend, thank you.' He stopped hugging Asim and looked up at the tower to where he'd been working not moments before, more than forty feet up. He was sweating profusely, like he'd been thrown into a bath and he stunk like the worst kind of odour you'd smell on a man. But that didn't matter. Asim was proud of what he'd done and both Sabrina and his friend stood and looked at Asim like he was some kind of a saviour sent from God.

The thankful man once more patted Asim on the back and just as they turned away to walk back to the camp site the man stopped Asim and his friend.'Hey, where are you going?' He said bluntly. 'You don't do something like that here and just walk away. Come inside, you're both invited into my home, after all you've just saved my life... or perhaps my legs from being broken, come, come.' He said with welcoming arms.

They walked through an open doorway and through a dark passage into a large room. It was the mans home and business. He asked them to sit down and walked to the side of the room to prepare some tea.

'Now where have you three strangers come from?' He asked as he poured the drink into small cups.


Leila was bored. Like her daughter Sabrina, she hadn't been out of the view of her tent in a week. She was more than grateful to not be walking any longer. God had handed them the gift of transport to the port town in Egypt, which had saved them weeks more of walking and tiredness. But she was now bored beyond belief. At least when they were walking they had a purpose, a daily goal. But now that daily goal was trying to wash and find food. It was boring and she wished so much for her old way of life. Not for the first time she reached into her pocket and took out one of the letters from her sister. Reading it to herself she relieved what tension resided in her. Every time she would look at the letter, she would finish by holding it to her heart, close her eyes and try to vision her sister working and living in Italy. The vision of her sister working behind a counter, passing clothes to a customer, or simply of her smelling a flower was something she envisioned regularly. It was always enough to invoke a hunger inside Leila, a desire to get up and be proactive. To not leave things to fate, but to take matters into her own hands. Once again it did the trick, she stood up, placed the letter back in her pocket and walked towards the tents entrance. She walked outside and looked up towards the sun. A calm, warm breeze swept over her and she could smell the saltiness of the sea. Not thinking of anything else, she walked away from the tent and towards the bottom of the site.

It felt good walking through the site. It was dirty and there were many people talking and generally not doing much. She didn't like what she saw and she, like her husband, realised in an instant they couldn't stay here much longer. They would have to get out of this place before it was too late. But one step at a time and today, she would regain that hunger for Europe and walk around. She wanted to see the Mediterranean for herself, get a lay of the land to see what was going on and perhaps find some kind of an advantage over everyone else here. She didn't know what it was she was looking for, however she knew that it was better than just sitting there in the tent, waiting for Jonathon to get back from wherever he was.

She continued to walk past the many tents, then looking down she caught a glimpse of the sea. It was there, still far off in the distance but there, just between the tents. She made her way to the bottom of the site and there it was, the blue of the Mediterranean Sea a mile away from her between scrubland and the tall metal fence. It was a distance away and obviously out of reach, but it was there and as she grabbed the fence with her hands. Once again she closed her eyes and thought of her sister in Italy.

From behind and out of her view, someone approached Leila. And as they did, Leila felt as the man placed his hand on her thigh. She turned quickly, shocked by what she felt and almost expecting to see her husband, however it wasn't. She turned and faced a man, who was staring at her figure, looking her up and down as if she were a piece of meat he desired.

She broke away from his gaze and his reach,

telling him to go away and leave her. However he again moved closer to her, reaching out his hand and attempting to touch her waist. She pushed his hand away and looked back where she'd come from. Then started to walk back up the hill towards the safety of her tent. At first the man didn't follow and she felt some relief when she looked back and saw him not following. Then she watched as he looked up at her and started to follow. She picked up the pace and started walking with more confidence and speed. She again looked back and watched him also pick the pace up. There weren't many people around, it was the middle of the day and most people were inside their tents, keeping out of the hot sun. She turned back once more towards where she was heading however was stopped in her tracks. Two other men stood in her way and she was completely blocked off from moving forward. One man grabbed her by the arm. He asked her where she was going in such a rush. Then with an amazing show of strength, pulled her towards his tent.

She fought to get away, shouting for help, but no one came out of their tent to help. It was one of many screams that people heard each day and most people kept themselves to themselves, not wanting to draw attention or get mixed up in anything out of their control. The second man placed his hand around Sabrina's mouth and she was dragged into the tent. Shortly followed by the man who'd originally touched her as she looked out at the sea.

He walked in and closed the entrance after him. Sabrina was pushed to the floor and continued to wriggle and fight her way out. But it was no good, the three men completely overpowered her and before long would get what they wanted.

As the two men held her arms she laid there, still wriggling and shouting, despite one man still smothering her mouth with his hand. She could do nothing, nothing was going to stop these men and with the realisation of her fate, she let out a cry, a plead for help. Tears running down her face as she continued to struggle. The man now standing above her, reached down and unzipped his trousers. As he pulled them down, he strode her, ready to take her for the piece of meat he desired. He reached down with his hand as a final act before doing the unthinkable. The two other men, still holding her arms, laughed at the sight of their companion getting what he'd set out to do. They had no regard for her and little regard for their friend, but it would be their turn next and they would each get what they desired. Leila was unable to defend herself and was at the mercy of the three evil men.

As she let out yet another scream the zip to the tent was yanked up and someone threw themselves in. Within a split second there was pandemonium within the tent as the scene unfolding in front of

Leila. A bat was thrown in the direction of the man on top of her. As it hit him, he flew to the side. Then shortly followed by the bat being flung in the direction of one of the men still pinning her arms to the side. None of the evil men saw it coming. It was a complete surprise to them that anyone was bothered by what they could hear through the tents thin lining. The man held out his hand and grabbed Leila's arm. He pulled her up and grabbed ahold of her side. As one of the men stood up, the bat was again flung in his direction and this time it connected straight on his head. He fell to the floor with a thump and laid unconscious, not moving. The man aimed the bat at the two other men who were trying to get up. Pointing his bat in anger, he pulled Leila to the exit. The men remained still, not moving, not wanting to receive another blow like their unconscious companion on the floor. Leila and the man ran out of the tent and walked upwards towards the top of the site. Leila was still shaking and as the man still grasped her arm, she tried to brake free. 'Wait, wait, I'm not going to hurt you.' The man said whilst holding her arms. My name's Omar and I work here. I remember you, you're Jonathon's wife, you came here only last week. Come, I'll take you back to your tent.' He said whilst escorting her back to the top, again taking one final look back down from the tent they'd come.

'Don't worry about them,' He said. 'I promise

you they'll not walk out of here alive.'

Omar walked Leila to the tent and waited with her until Jonathan came back. To Leila it felt like ages before he returned, but in reality it had only been minutes. On seeing Omar standing by her side, Jonathon realised straight away that something was wrong.

'Leila, what happened?' He asked as he watched her stand up and run for the comfort of her husband. He grabbed her and brought her in tight, fully embracing her.

'What happened Omar?' Jonathon asked him, looking him in the eyes.

'Three men attacked her whilst she was at the bottom of the sight. I didn't see completely what happened but by luck I was walking past as she screamed from their tent. If I hadn't have got there, I fear for what they would have done. She's okay Jonathon, she's shaken and has had an awful ordeal, but she's okay.'

Leila was sobbing in her husbands arms. He escorted her in and sat her down. He then walked back out and asked Omar who'd done this. Jonathon was angry. It was a measured anger, like someone who was in complete control of their emotions, but angry nonetheless.

'Don't worry Jonathon, I want you to stay here with her and keep out of trouble. I will sort this out.' He called out over his radio and told the man on the other line where to go and that he'd be there momentarily. 'Don't worry Jonathon, these men won't walk out of here alive, I promise you that. I will come back later.'

Omar placed a hand on Jonathon's shoulder. 'I have a proposition for you.'

As the afternoon went on, the three young adults sat in the comfort of the businessman's home. The man Asim had saved was truly thankful for the brave act which he'd witnessed and now they sat, drinking, smoking and talking about their lives.

The businessman was sympathetic to their situation in Egypt. He, unlike many of the people in the port town had an understanding of their situation and many of the circumstances which had brought them here. He understood that people wouldn't make the sacrifices they had, if it wasn't for a justified reason. And now sat down talking to the three young adults he realised they were genuine people. They weren't trouble, nor were they criminals like many of his township believed. They were genuinely running from dangers like he'd never faced before. He felt sorry for them, a pity that not many shared. He looked at Asim, it was a slow stare which seamed to pierce Asim's skin like he was trying to find something inside of his mind.

'You saved my life young man and I'm truly thankful. There's something I can do for you but it means you'll have to commit yourself to Egypt and not Europe. How about I offer you a job, working for me here. And not just you Asim, all three of you. The pay won't be great, but you can stay here, eat my food and build yourself a new life. Any person who saves the life of someone they don't know and in the means that you did, risking your own life, is worth having close to them. I owe you my life Asim, how about it?'

The man was genuine, he knew what he was doing in offering them a home, food and work. He was a clever businessman and knew that by employing people who were indebted to him was a clever thing to do. They would work hard and be loyal. But it wasn't just that. After sitting down for the best part of the afternoon and hearing Asim's story, he felt endeared to Asim and genuinely wanted to help him create a new life for himself, it was the least he could do.

Asim looked at Sabrina, then looked at his friend. Their minds had been made up already, they would start a new life here in Egypt.

# CHAPTER 16

It was late in the evening and for each person in the tent, the day had been mixed. For Sabrina and Asim it had been a day of realisation. They knew the opportunity they had was unique and that it was the right course of action for them both. For Jonathon and Leila, not including Sabrina's brother Damian, it had been a day of understanding of their surroundings and the situation they were in. This was a difficult time for them and for the time being they would count their blessings that Omar had been in the vicinity of the attack on Leila.

But now sitting together once again, they took comfort in one another's health and wellbeing, regardless of the ordeal Leila had earlier been through.

Sure enough, Omar had been true to his word. He'd met with one of his colleagues who worked under him. They'd gone into the tent and battered the three men to within an inch of their lives. For the man whom already laid unconscious on the floor, they continued to batter his legs to the point where every bone would be broken. They left him on the floor and the two other men lying next to them. Walking out, they told people in the local tents to not go in there, to stay away from that tent, it was marked. That night they would bring the truck by and deal with the three men once and for all. As Omar had once said, he kept order at the site and these three men laying down in a puddle of their own blood would be a reminder to all. Omar made the rules around here and no one should do anything to disrupt the flow of things.

After Omar had dealt with the three men in the tent, he'd gone and cleaned up, changing his blooded shirt and washing his hands. Later in the afternoon and after some careful deliberation, he went and found Jonathon to propose an offer of early transit to Europe. It was the offer of the three remaining seats on the next boat making the crossing. The idea of getting out of here was tempting, in fact more than tempting, however the fees were too great and the last thing Jonathon wanted was to annoy or anger the man who made the offer. With regret, but with a certain amount of dignity, Jonathon declined his offer, to which Omar accepted. However he did make it well known to Jonathon that he was not to mention this offer to anyone. It was a secret between the two men and that if news got out that he'd offered an illegal crossing to Jonathon, he would know where the news had originated. Omar kept his threat low key. He knew that Jonathon was a good man and he understood his reasons for not wanting to cross. So he left Jonathon and Leila to themselves in their tent. However he would keep a watchful eye on them. Despite his wicked side, Omar wasn't all bad, there was still a part of him that was both generous and caring.

The family sat together on the tent floor. Jonathon had mentioned that Leila had been attacked at the bottom of the site and told Sabrina that under no circumstances was she to go anywhere near the bottom. She would have to keep safe by staying within the local vicinity of their tent. He reminded Asim of his responsibilities and that as much as he trusted him with his daughters life, they should take nothing for granted. He'd explained that Leila had been attacked, but when Sabrina had asked what the attackers wanted, Leila had lied and said they wanted any possessions she had upon herself. Not only did Leila desperately want to forget the trauma of the afternoon, but she certainly didn't want Sabrina or Damian knowing what the men truly wanted to commit. She told Jonathon that he was not to tell Asim nor Sabrina and that he also was to forget about it. She was safe now and thanks to Omar, those men had been dealt with. 'Let's forget it Jonathon, let's move on.' She'd said to him. However Jonathon couldn't move on. His mind was taken back to when he'd brashly walked down the hill towards the militia compound and inadvertently placed Peter's father in danger. Every act that followed, whether good or bad made Jonathon second guess himself. On each occasion when he did, he was reminded of the sight of Peter's father falling to the ground, shot by the man who went on to destroy their town, their home and murder Asim's parents.

Since coming back to the camp site, neither Sabrina nor Asim had mentioned anything to anyone about the offer the businessman in the town had made. As excited as they were, they felt almost embarrassed to mention it and nervous at what Jonathon would say. Asim was also nervous at the prospect of being rejected. But as much as he was excited about the idea of staying in Egypt, he would also respect a decision made by Jonathon. Sabrina was after all his daughter and Asim would respect any decision he would make.

The time was right for Asim to bring it up. Sabrina was waiting for the moment, but up until this point hadn't found the moment nor plucked up the courage to say anything.

Asim started the conversation by telling them the story about the wooden scaffold tower which was close to collapsing and how he'd saved the businessman's life by climbing the tower and hooking the harness around a pole. Jonathon, wasn't one for bringing a man down, nor did he want to say anything negative. But considering what he'd been through earlier with Leila, he couldn't help but make it clear that perhaps Asim should have thought twice about putting his life in danger. Should the tower have fallen and killed him, who would have looked after Sabrina. Asim agreed that perhaps it was a little rash, but he went on to say that he took his guidance from Jonathon. That he would have done the same thing if he'd been in the same situation. 'Sometimes we put the safety of others ahead of our own. It's not always the right thing to do, but they are our first instincts. And they should not be ignored.We've been given this gift by God Jonathon and I saved the life of a stranger. I'm so proud of that.' He said.

"So am I father, Asim saved that man's life and he was so grateful. After the event had unfolded he took us into his home and looked after us. Father he's made us an offer.' Sabrina said whilst smiling.

Few too little times had Jonathon seen his daughter smile recently. There wasn't much to smile about right now, especially sitting here in the dirty old tent. He noticed her smile when she brought up the topic and he immediately sat up. 'An offer, what kind of offer?' He asked.

'After spending the afternoon with the businessman, he had an idea of the sort of people we are. He knows our story father and he's a lovely man. He was so appreciative of Asim's help, of his selfless act of heroism, that he's made us an offer. He'll take us both on to work for him and in exchange he'll allow us to stay in his home and share his food. He'll even give us a small wage. Father I know you want us all to go to Europe, but this offer is something else. I don't think we'll get a better offer.' She said looking him in the eyes.

Leila jumped into the conversation. 'But we've come so far darling, it's always been our plan to escape Africa and meet your auntie in Italy. There's a new life for us there already, we just have one final step to make.' Even though Leila loved her daughter more than words could speak, she could see in her eyes that her mind was already made up. Sabrina had always been a strong willed child and now older and even at child baring age, she was old enough to make her own decisions. Leila knew this, she'd been a similar age when she had met Jonathon and was equally as strong willed as Sabrina.

'Mother I know you wish to get across and I also wanted to move to Europe, however an opportunity like this may never come about again. And if it doesn't work out, we can always make the journey to Italy and meet up again. This isn't goodbye mother, father... Damian.' She said looking at her younger brother.

'Asim I don't know what to say. Are you ready to look after my daughter? To take her as your family, as your wife and to respect and look after her?' Jonathon asked.

'Yes I do father.' He said staring Jonathon in the eyes, being more serious now than he'd ever been in his life. It had been the first time he'd called Jonathon his father. Now felt the right time, regardless of it feeling a little awkward. But it was done and he could see the look on Jonathon's face the moment he'd said the word.

'Well then Asim. It sounds like your mind is made up, but of course I will have to meet this businessman you refer to. If he doesn't meet my expectations then... well let's just see. We'll find him in the morning.' Jonathon said.

Leila started to silently weep. Sabrina shuffled around to her and hugged her mother. 'What is it mother? Are you not happy for me?' Sabrina asked.

'Of course I am Sabrina, but Im losing my only daughter. This and the ordeal earlier, I'm just overwhelmed with emotions. I just wish we could get out of this place, it's awful. But I am glad for you Sabrina. To make a life in Africa, in Egypt will be good for you. Europe will be difficult, but it is the path we have chosen. I only wish we could get there sooner rather than later. Spending any more time in this camp than we need to is not going to be to our advantage. Jonathon can't you try and speak with Ahmed and see if he knows anyone.'

'I'll try, but we're going to have to wait, our time will come Leila.' He said whilst knowing he'd already turned down an early opportunity. This was another thing he was starting to second guess and it was made harder by the fact he couldn't tell anyone about it.

The following morning came and Jonathon walked into town with Asim early, before most people were up and walking around. It was the nicest part of the day. The sun had risen, however it was still cool. Birds were flying in the sky and there was a cool breeze that was whispering around. As they walked, Asim couldn't help but notice that Jonathon was quiet, more so than any other time he'd known him.

'What is it father? Why are you quiet?' He asked in a gentle tone. But Jonathon didn't want to talk about it. He wanted to honour the wishes of his wife and not tell Asim about the attack on her. But at the same time he wanted to talk to someone, to get it off his chest. He was torn with his loyalties, but also wanted to tell Asim and to warn him of the dangers of this place. He would need to be prepared if he were to look after his daughter when they finally made their journey to Italy and left them alone in Egypt.

Jonathon stopped in his tracks. 'Wait Asim, there is something I need to tell you about. But firstly you have to swear you will not tell anyone what I'm about to tell you, especially Sabrina.'

'What is it?' Asim asked, now sensing something big was on his mind.

'Leila wasn't attacked yesterday down at the bottom of the site. Well… she was attacked but.' He momentarily paused as he tried to get the difficult and traumatising words out of his mouth. 'She wasn't attacked for money or possessions, she was jumped upon and dragged kicking and screaming into a tent. Three men tried to… rape her. If it hadn't have been for Omar by chance walking past at that very moment, they would have gone through with it.'

Asim couldn't believe what he was hearing. He knew that both Leila and Jonathon had been quiet last evening, but he hadn't realised the magnitude of what they'd, Leila, had been through earlier in the day. He had no idea of what to say. He'd never been in this situation before where someone had just opened up to him like that. But if one thing over the previous few months had taught him, it was that life could throw things at you from all directions and that he should listen, observe and make judgement. Jonathon continued.

'Omar made us an offer yesterday. He offered us three spaces on a boat that's leaving tomorrow. I was so tempted to take it, so desperate to complete our journey. But I couldn't, I couldn't leave Sabrina or yourself here, not to mention the money. He asked for double what it would normally cost. Not only do we not have that, but we'd be mixing business with Omar and by all accounts he's not someone to mess with… he killed those men that tried to rape Leila.'

Asim was still intently listening, though now with his mouth gaping. 'I simply don't know what to say Jonathon. I had heard there were many boats crossing, not just the "scheduled" one's, but like anyone else around here, people don't seem to know anything about them. You only hear whispers from time to time. They must go on, but finding one. So Omar has something to do with the crossings?'

Knowing there was no one else around, Jonathon didn't mind talking freely about Omar. 'Asim you can not say anything about this to anyone. I am being absolutely serious here. Omar is a very dangerous person, by even mentioning his name in relation to crossing the Mediterranean, could get you beaten.

'So what did he say when you rejected his offer,

was he angry?'

'No, in fact he was understanding about it. He just reminded me to not talk about it to anyone. I think it's obvious he's doing it behind the back of Ahmed and making money on the side. It's just not something that we can afford. We'll just have to wait our turn, whenever that will be.'

'That could come sooner than later Jonathon.' Asim said. 'Jonathon how about I give you some money. You won't need much as you are saving money with Sabrina not crossing now. And I have money you can have if the offer is still open. Being that we'll have a place to live and food, not to mention a job, I won't need the money I was going to use for my own crossing.'

Jonathon stopped him before he could continue. 'I couldn't accept it Asim, that's your money, that's your future. I simply couldn't accept it. But thank you for the thought.'

'Jonathon I insist you take it. You have to get across now. You need to give Leila something positive before it's too late. You have to take advantage of this offer. God is looking down on you. This Omar, on the outside may appear to be a bad man, but to me, it sounds like he's been sent from God. It's his way. You should not look the other way. Take it, take my money and make the crossing, if it's still available.'

Jonathon paused, he didn't say anything for a few moments and the quietness was odd. He was never one for going quiet. He often spoke quickly, like he was somehow aware of what you were going to say next, but not this time. He was busy second guessing himself. The question of whether he should accept the money and the offer of an early crossing from Omar, or should he allow Asim to keep his money and bide his time before another crossing comes available? He just couldn't make up his mind, the decision seemed to be beyond him. Then before he could get his words out, Asim had taken the money from his pocket and placed it in his father's hands. 'It is your money Jonathon, make the crossing.' He told Jonathon with certainty in his order.

After Asim had taken Jonathon to the site where the scaffold tower had almost fallen, they went and found the businessman. Jonathon spoke to him and got a run down of who he was and what he did for a living. He came across as a very good person and he already had a certain respect for Asim. It was clear that he was somehow indebted to Asim for his heroism and that both Asim and Sabrina would be in good hands here in Egypt. Jonathon felt good for Asim, especially after everything he'd been through. It was wonderful for him to have hope again, to have something positive to look forward to. The fact that he had the opportunity to make a new life for himself and Sabrina was something that relieved Jonathon and now with the prospect of getting across to Italy sooner, things were starting to look up for them all.

First Jonathon would have to find Omar and hope he hadn't filled the last few spaces. Could it be they could be in Italy within a couple of days? Jonathon thought to himself. It was a thought that made him smile.

Despite the storm, Vicky and Michael had managed to get to sleep. The captain had been correct in his judgement of moving the cruise liner to calmer waters. The detour to calmer waters had taken around thirty minutes and after that, it was clear the water was calmer, still choppy, but calmer. It was enough to not further alarm the passengers and allow them to sleep in a fair amount of comfort.

The following morning came and the family all went to the main restaurant for breakfast. 'Now I understand why all the tables have lips over the edges, to stop things falling off when the boat tips upside down.' Belle said jokingly towards her mother.

Jude's ears pricked up when he heard his sister mention the boat turned upside down.

'Did it really go upside down?' He asked Vicky.

'No of course it didn't Jude, your sister was being silly. And don't worry, you fell asleep the moment your head hit the pillow. You would have woken up had it been that bad. The storm didn't last long.'

After going to the breakfast buffet, the entire family had their plates full with food from numerous counters. Vicky's first plate was full of fruit, with a small bowl of yogurt on the side. She always started her breakfast this way. It was her way of making it known to the family that she was watching her weight. But Michael knew the protocol here. She would always start this way and always ended up with a plate of eggs and bacon after. She wasn't kidding anyone. Michael already had his eggs and bacon on his plate and Belle wasn't far off with eggs and toast. Jude on the other hand had gone for the more sugary approach of a chocolate croissant, chocolate spread on the side and what looked like chocolate milkshake on the side of that. It was a normal morning aboard the ship for them and the other passengers, who by the looks of things were following the same approach. It would be the first of a few plates full of food they would consume every morning. They never went without.

Leila couldn't believe their luck. The attack on her from the previous day was far from her mind as she was set on getting her things together in a covert way. After Jonathon had spoken with Omar and accepted the last remaining seats on the transit to Europe, he'd told Leila to pack their things in a way that wouldn't raise suspicion with her old friends. They would have to get their things ready on the side and make their way out of the tent early in the morning before sunrise and whilst everyone else was asleep.

'Omar has made it very clear Leila that no one is to know where we're going. I can't stress that enough. He's done us a huge favour here and I don't want to get on the wrong side of him. Nor get him in any sort of trouble' Jonathon had said to his wife.

Sabrina was told about the family's early transit to Europe. She felt much more at ease with her new accommodation and job, knowing that her family would be equally settling to their new lives in Europe. In fact she wasn't just at ease with the situation, she was ecstatic with joy. After the turmoil of the previous few months, finally something good was happening to the family.

There wasn't much to get together. On leaving the village, they'd either sold most of their possessions or just given them away. They had very little to get together, it was all in a couple of small bags. But it was their life in the two bags, which they'd be carrying across the sea on their laps.

Leila had asked how much the earlier crossing cost, Jonathon had told her it wasn't much more and they could just about afford it, mentioning that Omar had helped them. Again, Leila couldn't believe their luck. Jonathon had agreed with Asim they would never speak of Leila's attack and the money he'd been gifted by Asim. They were secrets that neither of them would speak of again.

Everything was ready, even Sabrina and Asim were ready to leave the camp site months earlier than they'd expected. They'd spoken with the businessman and the three of them, which included Asim's new friend, would be moving in with him the next day. Firstly they would escort their parents to the coast and watch them depart for Italy the following morning.

Leila was fully packed and now, as the family sat together in the tent she looked across at one of her old friends, sitting on the other side of the large tent with her family.

Since moving into the tent, they'd not been that close. They'd spoken from time to time, but living together like this was difficult and the three families in the tent kept themselves to themselves. Now Leila looked over to her old friend, peering between the shoulders of Asim and Jonathon. Her friend was eating a meal that wouldn't have half fed her son Damian. It was still more than many people ate on the site. Starvation was one of the dangers of being here for too long. Frail malnourished people were far to a common thing here and it would be a happily forgotten memory when they left. The thought of starving, her son not having food in front of him was haunting. As she watched her old friend eating, she couldn't help but feel sorry for her. However her immediate attentions were for her family. That was where she focussed her thoughts, for her son and daughter. She, like Jonathon, couldn't believe that in a matter of a few days, she could be well on the way to meeting her sister. Once in Italy she knew it would still take a lot of effort to get to her sister, but at least they would be most of the way there.

Leila averted her eyes and looked at Damian. He was eating a small meal and talking to his father. Damian hadn't been told what was happening, Jonathon would carry him out of the tent whilst he slept. There would be no way of keeping their imminent move quiet if Damian knew what was happening. So they kept it from him, but he would know what was happening certainly when they left the camp site in the morning. Leila had decided not to eat anything. Not only was she feeling too excited to eat, but she also knew they would need food whilst on the boat. She had no real idea of how long they would be at sea for and how much food they could carry with them. But it more than likely wouldn't fit into their bags with their other belongings. So she would only be able to carry a small amount with her, on her person. But being they'd been on their feet for the past few months, not having much food was something she was used to. That deep, long, gutty groan her stomach regularly made was so common that she was used to forcing it to the back of her mind.

Vicky was now close to finishing her eggs and bacon. She placed some bacon on her fork and dipped it in the last of the ketchup on her plate. She ate the last of the bacon and wiped her mouth with a serviette. She screwed up the serviette and dropped it on her plate. She looked at Belle and then down at her plate which was still full of food. 'Are you finishing that Belle?' Vicky asked. 'It looks like your eyes were bigger than your stomach. Still it doesn't matter Belle, we're on holiday and it's all free.'

'Yeah I'm full up mum, I'm not going to finish it.'

'That was a waste wasn't it.' Jude sarcastically said.

Sarcasm was something that Jude had only recently picked up on and he regularly used it to annoy his sister. This holiday had been the perfect place to get used to annoying her. Jude had turned the corner from young harmless child to that of an annoying brother. It would be the start of things to come in their household and would start to wear thin at some point. But for now, Jude's sarcasm towards his sister was just a source of entertainment for his parents and they laughed when he commented on Belle's wasteful appetite.

They all stood up and walked back to their apartment. Their day would consist of eating their own weight in food, going to the local swimming pool, then spending the last hour of the morning on one of the lower deck bars overlooking the sea from a private balcony. It was the same lavish routine they'd done every day of their vacation so far.

Leila looked at Sabrina. She was so proud of her daughter and now they were about to be separated by the Mediterranean Sea, it would be the furthest away from her daughter that she'd ever been. But much like her husband, she felt proud, happy and excited. The fact they would be taking the most perilous journey of their lives was still far from her mind. As she said her final goodbye on the side of the beach, she let out a tear as she embraced her daughter for what would potentially be a long time. It would be months, if not years before they would see one another again and Leila was only feeling good thoughts. At no point did either of them admit to themselves that it may be the last time.

Sabrina hugged her father and brother. Asim embraced Leila and patted Damian on the head. Jonathon took Asim to one side and reminded him of his obligations. There was no doubt in his mind that Asim, though still young, would be more than capable of looking after Sabrina. If there were two things Asim had in his favour, it was his willingness to care for Sabrina and his work ethics. He was very able and could do anything, he would be an asset to this businessman and Jonathon looked forward to seeing him again in the future. He knew that when they would meet again, that Asim would be a man... and he would potentially be a grandfather. It was something Jonathon felt both proud and excited about. The future!

They all said their final words, holding hands until the final moment. Then came the shout from Omar standing by the boat, helping people get on.

It was an old ramshackle fishing boat, that had been converted long ago from a fishing boat to a transport vessel, illegally transporting people to Europe. 'Only God knows how many people this old boat has helped in the years it's been on the water.' Jonathon had said to Leila.

As they approached the boat, Omar looked at the two bags they were carrying, then looked at Jonathon. 'I'm sorry Jonathon, you can't take those, they'll make the boat too heavy.' He said looking at the number of people trying to board the small boat. Jonathon started to protest, however Omar was not joking.

'But these are our only possessions Omar, we can't leave without them, this is all we have from our old life.' He said now pleading with the man. Omar's voice took a different tone and Jonathon knew not to ask again. He turned to his wife, looking her in the eyes and taking the two bags from her hands. He then turned away and walked back over to where Asim and Sabrina were watching.

'These are your things now Asim, my son. We can't take them with us. This is all we have... all we had. Take them and do what you will with them. He handed the bags to Asim and in doing so the reality of his old life passing away was thrown into his mindset. He'd managed to keep those thoughts from the forefront of his mind, but in handing over his life long possessions, he now felt overwhelmed with emotions. Starting to well up with tears, he again hugged Sabrina and Asim. Then wiped his tears from his face before turning to face Leila and Damian who were waiting for him to board with them.

Jonathon walked over and climbed into the boat with his wife and son.

Omar watched as the boat slowly departed from the coastline. He had never gone on the boat to Europe, it was far too much of a risky crossing. He hated the idea of going on such a small boat and being in the open water. In fact, he'd never once set foot on the boat.

He watched as the boat was almost out of sight. The authorities would never find this small boat, it was far too early in the morning to be looking for boats attempting to cross the Mediterranean. They would get close to the Italian coast, then more than likely be picked up by the Italian Coastguard. The old ramshackle boat would be eventually released from the Italian authorities and be back here in a few days. It was always the same. As the boat motored further away he looked at the huge amount of money in his hands and was more than satisfied

THE JOURNEY

with himself for again filling the entire boat with African's.

Sabrina watched as the boat was almost out of sight. Asim was holding her hand and not once had she looked away from the boat or even said a word to Asim. Not even when he asked her how she was feeling. Sabrina was completely transfixed on the boat, watching, hoping they would make it away from the Egyptian coast without being stopped.

The minute the boat was out of sight, Sabrina turned to Asim. He wiped the tears from her eyes and gave her another hug. 'They will be fine Sabrina, they're on their way to a new life now... a new world on the other side of that sea.

Leila turned her attention away from the coastline. She could no longer see her daughter and Asim. She felt content at the prospect of their new life and equally for her own. She turned away and looked at her son who was watching the water as it washed past the boat as it motored towards the Italian coast. Damian looked around at his mother who was watching him and he smiled at her.

Leila smiled back at her son.

# CHAPTER 17

As the small boy desperately tried to keep ahold of it, the piece of debris constantly rolled as he struggled to gain any permanent grip. The chunk of wood was slipping out of the child's finger tips, then finally he felt his hand touch a small bar. Now grabbing the piece of wood with all his might, Damian was able to float without struggling to stay above the water. The piece of debris was just large enough to take his weight and yet still stay afloat.

As one wave after another crashed into Damian's face, he struggled to see the devastation of the what remained of the boat. Another wave splashed on top of him and again, he tried shaking the water from his face. However the onslaught was ferocious and he fought to see. Again Damian shouted his fathers name. This time he called his father by his first name in the hope that he'd be heard over the other screams and through the wind and rain. But Jonathon didn't hear his son.

As Jonathon was thrown into the blackness of the sea, he'd tried desperately to grab hold of some debris. There was a piece floating not two meters away from him and Jonathon could see it was close enough to try and grab onto. However like so many passengers on the boat, he couldn't swim. He was only staying buoyant by the clothes he wore and by his arms frantically trying to keep himself above the water.

The floating piece of wood remained two meters away from Jonathon, but just out of reach. As a large wave approached, Jonathon watched as the piece of wood rose first, before he followed in unison. Both climbing the steep wave, then both rolling down the other side. Jonathon could do nothing, he was completely at the mercy of the water and a few seconds later they were again rising up the steep slope off a wave. Back down again they rolled and straight into the path of yet another huge crashing wave. Only this time, the debris was the only thing still floating.

After ten minutes of shouting his father's name, Damian's voice was all but exhausted and his previous loud screams had been replaced by small whispers as yet more waves and rain reigned down upon him. He'd all but lost hope of seeing his mother and father again, however he continued to whisper their names.

As he rolled down the slope of a wave, another passenger bashed into Damian and the debris he clung onto. The woman had no time to react to the piece of wood being in her path and she floated by before being able to grab at any part. As the wave moved her past Damian she grabbed out and felt his leg. Feeling her grip his leg, Damian kicked out, knowing instantly that he was vulnerable. His grip was already starting to soften and any additional weight would pull him from the floating wood. As Damian's leg kicked out, the woman let go and was pulled away from him. From no where, Damian's grip was strengthened and again he rose to the top of the next wave.

Minute by minute, Damian noticed as the waves lessened and with them, the sounds of the shouting and wailing passengers diminished. One by one the passengers struggled to stay afloat and it wasn't long before their fight passed and they succumbed to the darkness of the sea. Their fate determined the moment they landed in the water.

Now no part of the boat remained on the surface of the water. There were a few small pieces of debris floating, the only evidence at all that a boat had been in the water. Only Damian and his piece of debris remained and they continued to rise and fall with the waves. Minutes went by and after a while Damian grew accustomed to the fact his parents and everyone else on the small boat were dead. But he clung onto the wood with every part of his might.

As the last of the waves departed behind him, Damian could see as the dark clouds were separating, leaving a star filled sky above. Now as the last of the clouds moved away, the moon shone on the water and glistened with every imperfection on the surface. The boy was now alone and at the complete mercy of the night. Damian had no idea if anyone would help him. He had no comprehension of what the coastguard was or even that other boats were in his vicinity. Having never seen the sea before this day, he had no idea whatsoever of its strength, of its utter dominance of anything it entertained.

Being saved never entered Damian's mind, in his opinion he thought he was already doomed. However, regardless of this, he never once thought of death. He had a strength that flowed through his body, both physically and mentally. He no longer felt scared of what would more than likely imminently happen. It felt like an inevitability that his grip would eventually loosen and that he would slowly drift asleep and with it he would again see his parents.

Damian continued to grip hold of the wood and he again looked up at the stars. They seemed to have a certain familiarity to them and he was reminded of being at home. The clouds in the background reminded him of the hills and mountains and for a while, he felt comfortable, like he could turn around and see his old home.

The warmth of the water around him licked at his jaw and felt comforting. Nothing feared him and his mind started to wonder… he started to relax.

# CHAPTER 18

The water was warm, especially as the temperature outside was just over thirty Celsius. The sun was blistering and not a cloud for shelter was in sight. Being the storm from the previous night had shook most of the Mediterranean area, it was a surprise to see nothing but blue skies. As the sun shone on the water it was reflecting into the eyes of Belle as she stared into her phone. Irritatingly moving from side to side, no matter which way she turned, there was a constant glare on the screen and before long, she'd given up hope of reading her messages with clarity. The only way she could've done so would have been to sit under an umbrella. But considering she wanted a good sun tan, sitting under an umbrella would have been counter productive. So she gave up hope, plus they'd be going down to the bar on one of the lower decks soon enough... it was part of their daily ritual.

Michael had torn himself away from the book he was reading and was playing in the water with

Jude. Up until this point Jude had played most of the time with other young children he'd bumped into in the water. It was a common thing for him to be outgoing and to sporadically start playing with random children of a similar age. It was one of his qualities and both Vicky and Michael knew that confidence would serve him well when he grew up. The two of them played so well together. Michael was still young at heart and enjoyed playing silly childish games with Jude. They had a good relationship together. Michael understanding when Jude needed his attention and Jude understanding when his father needed a sit down. But this time, they both played until exhausted, coming back to the sun beds and crashing down beside Vicky.

'Did you two have fun out there?' She asked whilst staring at her magazine.

'Yes, Jude's getting quite a swimmer now mum. Did you see him dive in earlier, he's got no fear of the pool. He must get that from you Vick!' Knowing full well she hated getting wet.

'Oh I'm not sure about that, I haven't swam properly for years Mike. Do those things really get passed down genetically?'

'You're crazy Vick, I wasn't being serious. He gets his confidence in the water from me of course, that and his good looks.'

'And of course he gets his brains from me.' Vicky said, still face down in her magazine. Michael bent over and casually lifted the front cover and tutted at the trashy celebrity story on the front.

'Yeah, I'm not sure about that!' He said whilst looking at the front cover in disgust and tutting. 'But seriously his confidence is improving in the water. I think he's actually enjoyed the water this holiday. It makes a change for him to not shy away from it. Anyway... shall we make our way to the bar, it's just gone eleven?' Michael asked.

'Yep, okay I'm ready for a pre lunch drink.' Vicky said as she placed her magazine in her bag and flipped over her sandals with her feet.

Like so many things on their vacation they had their various routines and going for a pre lunch drink was another of them. From the swimming pool, they'd all go straight back to their room and quickly get ready. A quick ten minute clean up then walk back over to the lift and head down a few decks to the balcony bar. The bar was situated on a huge balcony that overlooked the side of the beautiful white ship. Unfortunately the bar was on the starboard side and as the ship was moving to the East, they could only overlooked the sea, no land. But that didn't make any difference. They all enjoyed overlooking the sea and from their vantage point it almost felt like they were sitting on top of the waves, be it from thirty feet up. The boat was now a few miles off the coast of Italy and there wasn't much to see from the port side, so it made little difference which side the boat they were on today. But this was their usual pre lunch bar and they were already familiar with the staff, who always welcomed them personally by name. It was a speciality of this cruise liner that all staff made a point of remembering names, or at least acting as if they did.

The balcony was large and when fully seated it could hold just over a hundred people. However it was a huge ship, with plenty of bars, so at no point did the bar get anywhere close to being fully occupied. Again today, as the family sat down, there were no more than five families and a few individuals who were seated.

The waiter came over, he greeted the entire family by name and took their order, asking if they wanted their usual beverage. Both Michael and Vicky enjoyed an alcoholic Pina Colada, Belle had an orange flavoured non alcoholic cocktail and Jude another thick and creamy milkshake in a silver mixing jug. He never finished the drink, however both him and Michael did. His father always finished what Jude left, food or drink.

The family had grown closer again on this

holiday. They weren't exactly removed from one another when back at home in England. However with their usual busy lives, it was not uncommon to only catch up at the dinner table. But even then it was difficult getting Belle off her phone as well as getting everyone together at the same time. This holiday had been different and they all managed to talk and laugh at each other jokes and funny memories. Today though was the exception and they'd fallen back into their old ways. On seeing Belle back on her phone, Vicky had decided to pull out her trashy celebrity magazine and continue to read the article she'd stopped reading at the poolside. Like Belle, Michael was also staring at his phone and was catching up on the latest football news, leaving Jude to socially fend for himself. He didn't own a phone nor read well enough to enjoy a children's magazine, so he stared through the glass balcony. His confidence being at sea, had improved dramatically over the previous week and any bad thoughts he'd previous had, were almost diminished. When at the balcony, he often stood up against the glass and looked down the hull at the water as it gushed passed the steel outer lining. But today the ship wasn't moving at its usual pace. There had been a small engine problem, caused by the engine over working in the storm during the previous night. The staff were busy making adjustments to one of the ships drive engines and it would be another couple of hours before they ran at normal running speed. The liner would catch up on lost time during the night, ensuring they got to their next port on time.

Jude looked out to sea, spotting some rubbish and old wood drifting into the ships path. There was nothing of real interest to him and he gazed away back to the table. However on turning away, his gaze was caught by something else in the water. He took a closer look, focusing his vision on what it was that had made him look twice. In an instant, Jude's heart raced and a cool sweat appeared on his forehead. He stared in disbelief of his own eyes, almost choosing to disbelieve what he was seeing. Out there, not twenty meters from the hull was a small piece of wood, looking like a dot in the water. Hanging onto the wood was what looked like a small child, not moving but somehow hanging onto the wood. In that split second, Jude was taken aback to the vision of the news story he'd seen a year previous. The story of the dead child in the sea had come straight back into his mind. Only this time he didn't keep it to himself. Jude yanked at his fathers arm and shouted at him to look. Michael was fully engrossed in what he was reading and it didn't register with him that his son was uncomfortable.

'What is it Jude?' He asked, as both Belle and Vicky looked away from their distractions.

'Over there Dad, look, there's someone in the water... I think they're dead.'

Michael looked at his son and could see the fear on his face. His immediate thought, like that of Vicky, was that Jude had just spotted some rubbish in the water. Perhaps there was a swimmer, but immediately he dismissed the swimmer, knowing they were away from the coast.

Michael stood up and looked out. Sure enough there was indeed someone in the water. It wasn't clear straight away if they were alive, but they were hanging onto the wood with what looked like one hand. Michael shouted out at the bar staff to come over and sound the alarm. Then the person moved and it was clear it was a child. It was only a small, slight move of the child's other arm which was draped over the wood. Having been in the water for the best part of fifteen hours, it was all the youngster could muster. But it was enough for Vicky to see they were alive. Now a number of people had come over to the balconies edge and were watching as the small child gripped onto the wood as the boat slowly moved past. The heavy movement from the boat rocked the child and from no where their grip failed and they slipped into the water. There was no struggle, no kicking or waving of their arms in an attempt to stay afloat, the child just slid straight off the wood they'd been gripping.

Then not a moment later the youngsters head sunk under the waters surface.

## Twenty Five Years Ago

As Pat and Frank watched their daughter from high up on the balcony, they felt so proud of what she'd achieved. From pretty much not being able to swim five years ago, Vicky was now an accomplished swimmer and diver. She was at the pool non stop, every day she was practicing, both morning and night. It was unusual for a swimmer to partake in diving, but she did. Her coaches were really pleased with her and had tipped her as being a potential semi professional swimmer in the future. However they did openly admit she would have to put a stop to one of her events and solely commit to the other. It was the only way she would take the next step up in ability.

Standing on the top board, Vicky looked down at the water and concentrated on the small ripple on the surface. The ten meter board was something she loved the most, out of any other height and swimming stroke. The love of being on the top board, on her own, her destiny being in her own hands. It was something no other event could offer. She would never look up at the people watching nor look anywhere else other than where she was about to land. But in the split second she stood up on her tiptoes, there was a call from the crowd. Someone sitting next to her father stood up and shouted out her name. It was completely harmless, just a shout of encouragement. However it caught Vicky by surprise. As her knees bent, to gain traction and spring upwards, her knee buckled and what would have been a controlled and symmetrical jump, turned into something a less experienced diver would have performed. Immediately Vicky knew the trajectory she was on but there was nothing she could do, everything happened in a split second. Before she could react, Vicky had already committed to the jump and she landed, straight on her back. It was the biggest splash she'd ever made and everyone in the crowd gasped as they not only watched the poor girl hitting the water, but heard the smack as she made contact.

On hitting the surface, Vicky fell straight to the bottom and screamed under the water. It was the most painful experience she'd ever felt and she screamed with all her might. It must have been loud as most people heard her scream from under the water. Both Pat and Frank stood up, their hands cupped over their mouths as they waited the few seconds for their daughter to come up for air. Vicky swam upwards and awkwardly swam to the side. Her coach ran around the side of the pool and slipped as he turned the corner. Instantly picking himself up, he got back to his feet and shot over to the side of the pool where Vicky had swam to. He held out his hand and pulled her out. He looked at her back and could see it had gone bright blood red.

With one hand, Vicky leant on her knee as she limped over to the side. The coach waved at her parents to come down and could see they were already on their way over. They shot down the steps and carefully ran over to their daughter. Vicky was crying and still carrying the pain of the experience.

Before her parents had chance to say anything, her coach was already telling her what to do next. 'Vicky I hate to say this.' Her coach said. 'But you need to get back up on the board again, now. I've seen this before, if you don't do it now, it'll be harder for you in the long run. Believe me, I've seen this before. You need to get up there and forget about that. Prove to yourself and your subconscious that you can do it.'

However Vicky's parents didn't agree, they looked up at her coach in disgust, not believing that he could be so tactless and care free over what had just happened.

'She's not going back up there, Phil.' Frank said. 'Look at the poor girl, she can barely move.'

Vicky fought back the tears and looked at her

father. 'No Dad!' She said whilst wiping her eyes. I can do it, Phil's right.'

Vicky pulled her arm away from her father and looked up at the ten meter board. Wincing from the pain in her back, she attempted to stand up straight, however she was struggling. She limped towards the steps.

'Vicky you don't need to do this.We'll come back tomorrow.' Her mother said.

However Vicky had already blocked out everything and everyone, other than jumping off the board. She pulled herself together and climbed the steps to the top.

Arriving at the top she continued to make her way forward. Her many years of experience were acting like muscle memory as she continued to move to the edge, fighting against her recent memory. She looked over the edge and closed her eyes. Moving into the preparation stance, she was one tiptoe away from jumping. Her parents both watching from directly below the board, again with their hands over the mouths. The crowd clapped in unison, to give the young lady further encouragement.

Vicky stood there, almost ready to jump. One second went by, then two, three, four. She just couldn't do it. Despite her wanting to jump, she just couldn't do it. Her memory of falling, of the pain still searing through her entire body was all too real. Vicky's subconscious would not allow her to jump, to dive into the water like she'd successfully done not ten minutes before.

Vicky closed her eyes and fell backwards, ensuring that she didn't go anywhere near the water. Landing on her bottom, she pulled her knees upwards and sat huddled on the floor in the middle of the top balcony. She didn't move from that position until her father approached her. He sat down next to her and placed his arms around her. The crowd all quietly whispering how sad it was, and all hoped she would be okay.

'I just couldn't do it Dad. I wanted to, but my mind would't let me. Can we go home?'

That was the last time Vicky dived into the water. In fact it was the last time she partook in any activity in the water. She'd struggled to pluck up the courage and make her way back to the pool. Even just for a casual swim with her friends, Vicky had known that seeing the board would bring back the pain of that fateful fall. Even swimming on holiday was difficult, although the proceeding years to follow would get easier. But she vowed never to go near a spring board again. It wasn't until taking a younger Belle to her swimming lessons, that she even looked at a swimming lane or diving board.

As the young child's head sunk beneath the turquoise water, no one could do anything other than gasp. The alarm from the cruise liner had sounded, but it would be a good few minutes before anyone could get down there to save the child.

Vicky boldly stood up and started to take matters into her own hands. She flung off her sandals, took off her shawl and shorts until she was only wearing her swimming costume.

'What the hell are you doing Vicky?' Michael barked. 'What the hell Vick, you can't…' But before he could say anything else or raise his arm, Vicky had already readied herself to jump. It was the most reckless thing she could do. But it was all that could be done for the small child and any further delay would see the child sink to their death.

Within a split second, Vicky had climbed over the glass barrier and jumped. She didn't think anything, other than trying to jump away from the ships hull. Her motherly instinct for a child's safety took over every other instinct she had for her own safety and wellbeing. As she fell towards the waters surface, she thought nothing else other than the child's safety. Everything had happened so quickly and it hadn't been not twenty seconds since the child's grip had failed them. Entering the water, Vicky instantly realised she'd splash landed and hadn't felt any pain. The painful feeling of twenty five years previous was a long distant memory. Now under the surface, she opened her eyes and saw the child straight away. With immense speed and agility she swam a few meters deeper to get a grip on whatever she could. Everyone watching from the balcony and from the top of the ship, watched with their mouths open as they couldn't believe what this women was doing, how courageous she was acting. Many people stood there watching and recording the moment on their cell phones.

Holding the child tightly in her arms, Vicky breached the surface and was treading water to stay afloat. 'It's a boy and he's alive.' Shouting up to whoever was listening.

Damian was still conscious but had little energy, it had been barely enough just to have held on for as long as he did. But he had enough to open his eyes and look into Vicky's, if only for a split second. It was at that moment that Vicky had realised the boy was alive. She shouted in joy at the reality of this miracle and continued to shout to people on the now stationary ship.

A few short moments passed before a small motorised dinghy came around the ships bow and pulled up against Vicky as she trod water with the boy in her arms.

'That was the most brave thing I've ever seen.' Said one of the men wearing a lifejacket and pulling Damian from the water. The man rested the boy carefully on the floor, took off his shirt and placed a foil jacket over him. Another man reaching over and also pulled Vicky up onto the boat. Not a few seconds later, they were already speeding around the ship to where they'd dropped the dinghy into the water.

Michael, Belle and Jude couldn't believe what happened. They'd watched the entire episode unfold and were both in shock and also in complete awe at what their mother and wife had just done. None, especially Belle could believe what her mother had accomplished. She had no idea that her mother, "a tired old house-wife from the UK" could jump into the sea from such a height and save a boy from drowning. Being escorted by a fellow member of staff, the three people jogged through the ship to the other side where they would be reunited with Vicky and the exhausted child. Michael and Jude led the way with Belle slowly keeping up. She'd completely forgotten about her phone which she'd left on the bar table. Now struggling to keep up with her brother and father, she was still trying to process what had occurred only a few moments before.

It felt like ages before they arrived at the port side of the ship and in doing so, they watched as the small dinghy was winched back up to the deck where they were standing.

'Mum!' Jude shouted as he watched his mother cradling the small boy in her arms. Vicky looked up at the three of them and smiled, then looked down at the boy she'd rescued. Damian had been given something sugary to drink and already, he was starting to gain more energy. As Vicky stared down at him and smiled, he knew he was safe and alive. But he felt scared and utterly confused. In the moments that followed, it almost felt like being born again. Being pulled from the water, from where his mother lay, then being brought into this new world. He'd never seen a white woman before, never in person and only in a few pictures, it felt strange and alien to him. However he thought nothing else about it. This person who was caring for him felt comforting and warm and more than anything he felt safe.

One of the men took Damian and carried him off the dinghy and onto the deck of the cruise liner. He rested him on the floor and up against the side and stood by until the medics came. Vicky again sat down next to him and cradled him. Damian rested into her chest and once more allowed his muscles to loosen and again he relaxed.

Michael leant over Vicky and kissed her forehead, he then placed a warm, comforting hand on Damian's forehead.

'He'll be okay Vick... thanks to you and your heroics. I just can't believe you did that. I should have stopped you, you could have died. But my God!' Michael just shook his head in utter disbelief at what had occurred, still not fully comprehending the situation. It was only twenty minutes ago they were leaving their room for the lift to take them down to the balcony bar and now look at them.

Belle also bent over and kissed her mother. It was the greatest show of emotion and affection she'd shown her mother in years. 'Mum you're a hero.' And as Belle looked down at the tired child in her arms, she started to cry.

'Oh Belle, don't be sad, he'll be okay.' Vicky again said whilst looking down at him.

'I'm not sad Mum, I just can't believe that you had it in you. For a second I thought you were in trouble when you didn't surface straight away. But on seeing you rise out of the water with him in your arms... I just couldn't believe it.' Belle said whilst wiping dry the tears from her eyes.

Jude was just staring, transfixed on Damian and he felt as if he'd been in this situation before. The memory of the dead child, face down in the sand was well ingrained in his mind. But now this had occurred, he felt like it was all true, like a deja vu. But only this time, the child was alive and in his mothers arms. Jude looked at the boy and the two of them caught one another's attention.

In typical Jude fashion, he sat down next to the child and placed an arm over his shoulder.

'My name's Jude.' He said smiling at the young boy.

# CHAPTER 19

One week after Sabrina and Asim had seen off their parents from the beach and Sabrina was feeling a little concerned she'd not heard anything from her parents. Asim had given them both a telephone number for where they could find them, provided by the businessman, Maat, and since the moment they'd seen them off, they'd been waiting for a call or message to say they were in Italy. But nothing had come, no messages nothing. Omar had done Jonathon another favour in allowing both Sabrina and Asim to watch and just told them they had to keep it to themselves and that he wanted nothing further to do with them. They were never to search for him nor even mention his name. They'd both agreed and were thankful to have been enabled to see them off. Jonathon had warned them of Omar and told them never to cross him, he wasn't to be messed with. But after a week of impatient waiting, they were now at the point where they were getting desperate for an answer.

Sabrina was busy working as a waitress in

one of the Maat's restaurants. Although she was finding it difficult understanding what some of the people were ordering, being they both spoke a foreign language. However she was getting by and learning the whole time. Maat was pleased with the work she'd done and more than happy with their agreement.

Asim and his new friend Ali, mostly worked together and like Sabrina, were getting on well and more than enjoying their new lives. They were either reluctantly working at the top of the scaffold tower repairing and painting Maat's building or working washing dishes or cooking in his restaurant. And similar to that of Sabrina, Maat was please with how they'd adapted to working full time. At no point had Maat regretted his decision and now, only a week into their employment, he was already finding himself trusting each of them. He couldn't have asked any more of them and likewise, they respected and honoured Maat by working their hardest to repay their gratitude.

Ali, who had previously been at the campsite for the best part of six months, had said his goodbyes to his two friends who he'd shared a tent with. They were both older than him and accepted that he wanted to do something different. Their journey's had started months before that of Ali and their hearts were set on reaching Europe. So when Ali had told them of his offer to stay and work in Egypt, they were only pleased for him and wished him luck. But after leaving them at the site he'd not seen them since. But he always looked out for them when he was up at the top of the scaffold tower. With one eye on his work and the other on the nearby market, he hoped to see them just once. If anything, he wanted to give them something as way of thanks for their hospitality, safety and for looking out for him after they initially met during their previous failed crossing. After that point they'd been his only family. It had been a difficult thing, saying farewell to them, but they all understood it was for the best.

Now at the top of the tower alone whilst Asim was grabbing them some lunch from the kitchen, Ali was taking five minutes from working. Despite having an old white canopy over the top of the tower, it was still hot up there. Ali picked up his water bottle with one hand and took a swig, his legs rested and dangling over the side. He placed the lid back on the bottle and looked down at the ground thirty feet below. He was reminded of the moment the tower had collapsed last week and that if it wasn't for that failed knot in the rope pulling the tower tight to the wall, they'd all be sat down in the campsite playing cards. Ali couldn't believe their luck and often prayed, to say thanks for the accident that never was.

He placed the bottle down and as he did, he caught sight of both of his old friends from the site. Shouting down to them to get their attention before they walked past the side street he was on, he caught their attention. They both looked up and pointed at Ali, then ran over to the bottom of the tower. Ali shot down the tower faster than he'd ever got down before and greeted them with open arms.

'My friends!' He shouted. 'I've missed you both, how are you?' He asked with a huge grin on his face.

'We can't be long Ali, in fact we've come here looking for you.'

'What is it? I've so much to tell you.'

'We shouldn't be telling you this and you can't mention it to anyone how you found out.' One of the men said quietly, not trying to attract attention.

'What, what?' Ali again asked.


Asim had picked up both his and Ali's lunch from the kitchen and was bringing it back over to the tower where they'd eat it at the top. They enjoyed this time of the day. It was busy below in the market and they had the chance to look at people as they went their daily lives. The realisation of them both working fully time jobs hadn't fully sunk in yet and they were both still enjoying being busy, being useful and appreciated by someone.

As Asim approached, he looked up at the top of the tower and Ali was standing, looking over the side towards the sea. His blank stare over the buildings towards the sea looked different to Asim, as if he were troubled or just in careful deliberation about something. Asim didn't shout up to Ali, he just made his way up and stood next to his friend.

'Here you go Ali!' Asim said whilst passing his friend his lunch.

'Thanks Asim. Listen.' He said whilst still contemplating how to break the news to him. Ali knew he had to break the news to Asim and Sabrina straight away, this couldn't wait… But it would break their hearts.

Practically jumping down the scaffold tower, Asim landed with a thump at the bottom as he swung down front the final level. He ran around the corner, leaving his friend behind who was still at the top and feeling sick from breaking the news to him. Telling him where the news had come from and that Omar had told his friends to find him so he could equally pass on the news to Asim and Sabrina.

Asim continued to run towards the restaurant where Sabrina worked. It wasn't far, no more than a quarter mile away and it gave Asim the time he needed to work out what he would say to Sabrina. As he shot around the final corner, he caught a glimpse of the restaurant. He ran over and violently pushed the door open. Everyone in the restaurant looked up from their food and stared at Asim as he was panting for air. Sabrina was stood in the middle of the restaurant with a tray of drinks in her arms.

'Asim, what are you doing here?'

'Can we talk Sabrina, come round the back. Sorry everyone.' He said to the customers whilst quickly walking around the back to the kitchen.

'Asim you're sweating, have you ran all the way here?'

'I have Sabrina. I have something to tell you, it's about the boa that took your family, our family to Italy.'

'What Asim?' She tried rushing the news out of him.

'The boat didn't make it to Italy. In fact the boat hasn't turned up at all... anywhere. Omar can't contact the captain and hasn't heard anything from his contact in Italy.' Asim could see Sabrina's normal cheerful expression had been replaced by that of a stone cold expression with nothing but fear on display, her eyes staring coldly at his. 'The boat went down in a storm Sabrina and there are no survivors. I, I'm so sorry?'

Sabrina collapsed to her knees. She didn't scream, knowing it would upset the customers. But she was crying and she cupped her face with her hand and cried profusely. Asim got to his knees and cuddled her.

After what felt like minutes, she looked at Asim. 'Have you seen Omar then, who told you about this?'

Ali's friends from the site found him whilst I was out getting lunch from the kitchen fifteen minutes ago. They'd been given a message from Omar and were told to find Ali and pass the news onto you. We're not to make contact with him though, apparently he was very clear on stating that. This was something he did out of respect for your father Sabrina. We've been fortunate to hear this news at all.

Sabrina again started to cry. In questioning Asim over where the news had originated, she placed a small amount of hope that the news had come from hearsay, maybe it had been another crossing. But on hearing that Omar had passed on the news, it was clear it was true and there were no survivors.

'I have to work Asim.' Sabrina told him. Her

resilience and strength was something he'd not witnessed from her before. Wiping the tears from his own eyes, Asim stood back up.

'There's nothing we can do Sabrina. I just…' The words couldn't get out of his mouth. Sabrina was already standing and straightening her clothes. She noticed he was also crying and embraced him.

'Asim go back to work, we'll morn them tonight.' She ordered.

Asim walked out of the restaurant and headed back towards where Ali was already back working. He was walking slowly and giddy like, as if he was drunk. The moment he heard the news, he thought of nothing other than telling Sabrina. He'd had no time to think of the reality of the event and what had happened, the fact he'd lost his second family. He paused for a moment and rested a hand against a wall. Asim went cold all over and started to get a cold sweat come over him. Then before he noticed, he fainted to the floor.

Sabrina had straightened her clothes and ordered Asim to go and continue with his work. This job was the most important thing in their lives. Doing a good job both housed and fed them and keeping Maat happy was the only thing that mattered. But that didn't stop her from taking one more moment to stop and collect her thoughts before walking back into the busy restaurant.

Sabrina and Asim had both mourned the loss of their parents the same night. They went down to the sea after dark and lit a candle in her parents memory. She felt exhausted like no other time in her life. On her parents leaving for Italy, she knew full well it would be years when she would again see them. Sabrina had resigned to the fact she would have to fend for herself now, there was no relying on her parents for anything. It was her and Asim now and she was already, only a week after her family had left, coming to terms with that fact. So on hearing the news from Asim, she hadn't reacted as perhaps she would have done weeks before that. It didn't stop her from crying once more with Asim on the beach as they sat side by side staring into the darkness of the Mediterranean Sea.

Over a month had gone by since hearing the news of her family's fate. Sabrina had all but come to terms with the fact she would never again see her parents. She often spoke with Asim about it, never keeping things bottled up. He cried more than she did, he seamed to take it far worse than she had. But then he'd also lost his own parents and best friend all in the last few months and Sabrina knew his losses were far more than her own. She felt lucky she had Asim, he was hard working and loyal and they would have a long life together. Sabrina knew that without him, she wouldn't be where she was on this day. In fact she thought she might be dead, especially as he'd looked after both herself and Damian the night their village was attacked. He was a good man and she would be the perfect wife for him, when the time was right to get married.

The end of the day was when Sabrina felt the pain of loss the greatest. During the day there wasn't enough time to grieve, certainly not the time to spend time thinking about her loss. She was always on her feet, whether tidying up from breakfast, walking to the restaurant or standing up taking orders and bringing people their food. Often she would see another young child and be reminded of her brother. However it was always a passing thought and only a few seconds would go by before she was thinking about other things. It wasn't until the evening time when she had more time that she found herself thinking of her family. After all, they always spent time together at night, so it was only natural for her to miss them most at this time.

Since understanding the loss of her family, the grieving had become easier. But more so after a few weeks and now every day felt a little easier. Sabrina wanted to go and find Omar, to ask him face to face what had happened. She couldn't help but think that his crossing, being more secretive than most others, had been the reason they died. Asim had mentioned that perhaps it was an older boat, perhaps one which was used by criminals and was ramshackle, not seaworthy. But the moment he mentioned it, he wished he hadn't. He knew that Sabrina was strong willed and that Jonathon's point of not mentioning Omar's name in relation to crossings or seeking him out, would be lost on her. She would always do what she wanted, especially if she thought it was justified. Asim new that his words would act as tinder on a fire and he quickly tried retracting his thoughts. But it was no good, Sabrina had already made up her mind and was going to seek him out the next time she had a day off.

Asim had mentioned it to Ali and he'd strongly advised against it, claiming that he'd seen first hand some of the things that Omar had done.'He's really not a good man Asim.' He'd said, telling him to beg, insist that Sabrina doesn't go anywhere near him.

But on every time that Asim mentioned it to Sabrina, she flatly refused and said she'd go anyway. Asim was very concerned at the prospects of her finding Omar. So he did the only thing he could do and speak with Maat. Maybe he knew Omar, or knew of him by reputation. However when speaking to Maat about Omar, he agreed with Ali. 'He's clearly not someone to get involved in. If he's deeply involved in such crossings and taking all that money, he's clearly got a lot of dangerous people behind him. If someone was to get caught by the authorities and their crossings were stopped, then whoever was to blame would be killed. These people don't mess around. I will speak with Sabrina later and try to discourage her.' Maat said to Asim. 'She's at my other restaurant today cleaning up after the builders finished the new kitchen, the place is a mess. I'll head over there a little later and talk to her, leave it with me.'

Sabrina was busy shifting rubbish out of the newly built kitchen. Like so many tradesman in the area, they were so messy. Building was their trade, it most definitely wasn't cleaning up after themselves. The moment she walked through the front door she could smell dust and dirt in the air. There was a lot of work needed before Maat could start serving food to people. But she liked the look of this place and hoped that perhaps she could work here sometimes, just to have a change of scenery. Finding a pile of bags on the floor, she unfolded one and started throwing rubbish in. There were cans everywhere, dirty bottles and piles of old bricks and dust. The entire place was a health hazard.There were old newspapers on the floor, some had old food wrapped up and others looked like they'd be used to sit on. Picking up one paper she opened it, wondering if she could read any of the words. She was starting to understand what people were ordering and made a point of speaking the language. However reading was something completely new to her. Picking up the paper and opening it her mouth dropped and her eyes widened. The entire page was showing a white lady on a boat carrying what looked like Damian. She couldn't read any of the words and had no idea what was happening. It was clearly a new picture or at least fairly new. She looked closely at the picture and realised it was without doubt her brother. Sabrina screamed with exuberance, the excitement of this like nothing she'd felt before. She dropped what she was doing and ran out of the door, closing and locking it behind her. Then ran as fast as she could to find Asim. She was running so fast she ran into people, knocking one you man to the ground. She shouted her apologies and carried on running with the scrap paper in her hand.

As she approached the building where Asim and Ali were working she was already shouting Asim's name. She hoped he would hear her and run out or down from where ever he was working. She reached the bottom of the old scaffold tower and looked up, but Asim wasn't there.However he had heard her shouting his name from the top of the street and was walking out of the building when he saw her staring at the bottom of the tower looking upwards for him.

'Sabrina!' He said. 'What is it, what are you doing here?'

She flung the paper in his face. 'He's alive Asim, Damian's alive.'

'What? How… That's him Sabrina, that's him in the arms of that lady. Here, come with me.'

Asim took Sabrina inside of the building and found Maat, asking him to read the paper for them. After reading the entire article on the miracle child that had been found at sea. Maat pulled out his smart phone and typed in some of the information from the paper. Sure enough he found more details of the miracle child and found a video of the event unfolding. Sabrina had grabbed the phone from Maat's hands and understanding the situation, he didn't mind her boldness in doing so. She watched the entire thing. Someone had recorded this woman diving into the water and saving the child. Their were loads of different videos from different angles and on each, Sabrina could see that Damian had been saved just at the moment his grip had given up on him. This lady who'd saved him was a hero.

Sabrina finished watching the video and again, fell to the floor and sobbed. She just couldn't believe that he was alive. However her tears weren't solely for joy, it was also clarification that what

Ali's friends had said, about her family perishing, was indeed true. The months of grieving that had started to ease, had just hit her like a ton of bricks and she could think of nothing else but to collapse and breakdown in emotion.

Through the tears, Sabrina turned around and looked at Maat. He looked down at her. She looked so beautiful, but yet so troubled. He hoped that his children would never have to go through what this poor girl in front of him on the floor had. He would do what he could to help Sabrina. For some strange unknown reason to him, he felt a heart wrenched obligation towards her.

'What now Maat, how can I find my brother?' Sabrina asked.

After Damian had been rescued and the vessel's engines had been patched up, the ship moved on towards its next port in Naples. Already Vicky's life had been changed and she was treated more like a minor celebrity for the remainder of the journey. Dining with the captain and having free rein of the ship. However it was the last thing on her mind. She had no care for any of the pleasantries and just wanted what was best for Damian. He was talking and had spoken to someone on the ship who spoke his language. He was very thankful to Vicky for her heroics, but was very unsure of what was happening. He chose to stay with Vicky and her family in their cabin on the ship, which had been upgraded to the largest on the ship.

After the cruise liner had docked and the media had finished talking to Vicky, she had opted to stay with Damian in Italy until they knew what was happening. It was clear that he had no immediate family, his mother and father drowning at sea, however he had mentioned that his aunt was living in Italy and had a sister in Egypt. Neither his aunt nor sister had been found and people wondered whether he knew what he was saying. So it had been discussed numerous times that he might be best placed in a children's home indefinitely or at least until family came forward. However Vicky, who'd taken it upon herself to look after the child, would not allow this, it would be an absolute last resort. After a few weeks, Michael, Jude and Belle had gone back to the UK, leaving Vicky in Naples to help try and find Damian's auntie. But it was never far from her mind that he might be best going back to the UK. They never wanted three children, but this was something completely out of the ordinary. Never before had they been involved in anything like this. However the family had proved themselves. They'd all cared for Damian, even Belle. When they left Italy for the UK, they'd all been upset at leaving Damian behind, believing it would be the last time they'd ever see him.

After a month, hope was looking lost and the media had started to lose interest in the search for Damian's aunt. It wasn't until a phone call from someone in Egypt, there was a resurgence of interest. As if by complete luck, Damian's sister had come forward. She'd had no idea her brother was still alive and was making her way to Italy to be reunited. However she was struggling to get over because of not having a passport. It was not going to stop her and with the help of Maat, she was making headway in her pursuit of getting to Italy. Though she swore to Maat that she would return, stating that Egypt was her new home.

'I spoke to Damian again today Asim, but it's strange talking to him on the phone, he doesn't sound like himself. He needs me there. Vicky is being kind to him and staying with him, but he needs me there, I can't wait any longer to get over there.' She said, feeling anger at the length of time it was taking.

Days felt like months as she made her way through endless amounts of paperwork and bureaucracy. But finally she was getting somewhere, now all she needed was a flight… No one was getting her anywhere near a boat!

Standing in the airport waiting lounge, Vicky was holding the hand of Damian. Communicating was initially difficult, however the two of them had their own mutual understanding and they both stood there as planes were taking off and landing. Damian had never seen a plane up close and the experience had been a pleasant interest to him. Damian's aunt hadn't been traced yet, despite Sabrina knowing the city she was in and her name. However like so many African's who came to Italy, they often changed their surnames to Italian one's to assist in finding work. So it was proving more difficult than Vicky first imagined, however they continued to search.

As Sabrina's plane landed and moved closer to the terminal, Damian was showing signs of excitement and when people started to walk through the entrance to the lounge, he pulled his hand from Vicky's and ran over. Vicky ran after him and stood by him as he watched people coming out. None of them knew the significance of this small child standing in their way and many people were frustrated at this boy standing in their path. Vicky pulled him gently back and they waited. Damian's head moving quickly above and to the side of the oncoming people as he watched eagerly with anticipation. After a few minutes there was still no sign of Sabrina. Then Damian saw her walk around the corner. She also caught sight of him and ran over. Sabrina threw her bag on the floor and hugged her brother with every bit of strength she had. The two of them embraced like never before until Sabrina let him go. She looked at Vicky who'd been crying at watching the two siblings reunite. She held out her hands and the two of them embraced.

'Where's Asim? did he come?' Damian asked. Sabrina looked over her shoulder, back to the boarding gate, wondering where Asim was. He'd got held up behind some other people who were taking their time getting off the plane. On seeing Sabrina and Damian together, Asim ran the length of the corridor towards them.

'Damian!' He shouted. 'I never thought I'd see you again.'


After weeks more of searching, Damian's aunt was eventually found living and working in Rome. She'd taken on the surname of Romano, Serena Romano. She was thirty five and had a husband and children. She worked in a shop just outside of the city and despite seeing Damian in the news and on social media, she hadn't event contemplated he was her nephew. It wasn't until Sabrina had come over to Italy and the two of them had finally met up, that she realised they might be related. After all she'd never met Damian. She'd left home when Sabrina was only five, a few years even before Damian had been born. After moving away, she had managed to send a few letters back to her sister, however only once did she have a reply. She assumed that Leila didn't want to reply, perhaps because she was angry that she'd left her behind when she went to Italy or that she was just not receiving anymore letters from her. So she'd stopped sending letters, plus contacting by phone was impossible where Leila's family lived. The two of them had lost contact and Serena's hope of seeing her sister had all but diminished. But not Leila's, she always had it in her mind that she wanted to go to Italy and make a new life there. It was just a shame Serena hadn't known how her sister felt.

When Sabrina was reunited with Damian, Serena was dumbstruck when she saw them on the news. She instantly recognised Sabrina. She still had the same beautiful features she'd had when she was younger. There was no doubt in her mind that she was her niece so she made the telephone call to the authorities before making the 3 hour journey to Naples. On arriving she felt nervous and scared of what her niece might say. Feeling that she might be angry that she hadn't come forward sooner. However her fears were far from the truth.

On hearing that her sister had desperately tried to come to Italy, giving her life for the effort, Serena felt awful. She felt that she could have done more, she could have sent money back to her family to get them a flight to Rome or perhaps made the journey back home herself, if only to holiday. However that was in the past and her life in Rome was good. She had work, her children were at a school and they had a modest home. There was little additional money to vacation and her immediate concerns were for her family. For the previous eight years, Leila and her family were out of touch and... living a life in a whole different world. But Serena had never stopped thinking of her sister. She just never thought she would make the perilous journey across the Mediterranean that so many African's made each year. All for the purpose of what they believed would be a better life.

The question over Damian's needs were made clear from the moment Serena arrived in Naples. She spoke a small amount of English and spoke with both Vicky and a translator about his immediate needs. She couldn't believe the courage that Vicky had shown in jumping into the sea to save a stranger. She was grateful of the fact that she'd stayed with him this entire time, putting her families needs second ahead of this child she'd only met a few weeks before.

Since arriving in Naples, Vicky's life had been turned upside down and her old life back in England, felt so far from where she was now. Vicky, like so many other people, simply didn't appreciate what people went through when they were making the journey to Europe. The reasons why and how were often kept from the people. Only on occasions were the real reasons mentioned, whether persecution, famine or war. Mostly people thought it was solely for money, to have what they desired, the life of a Westerner. However, Vicky had quickly found things were far different than what she'd previously learnt through solely watching the news or reading an article online. Now here in Italy and seeing first hand what people were doing to get to Europe, her beliefs and understanding of the situation had been turned upside down and were entirely changed. She vowed to change her life, to do something that would make a difference for these people. But what that would be she had no idea. One thing she was certain of, was that in that act of heroism, her old life had died and she'd been reborn in Italy.

For Damian, it was clear that he needed to be with his family. The offer from Vicky and her family was amazing and very appreciated, however he needed his own family. Sabrina and Asim had initially put the idea forward that Damian could go and live with them back in Egypt. Though considering they were only young themselves and were busy getting their new lives on track themselves, it would be difficult for them to concentrate the right amount of time and energy into Damian's upbringing. It certainly wouldn't be for the want of trying, however it would be just too difficult. So the only option was for him to stay with his aunt and her family. It was the life that her sister had wanted for Damian, to move and be brought up in Italy, it was what she wanted and clearly what her wishes were. Serena was prepared to do what was necessary. Damian would live with her in Rome.

## Ten Years Later

'Come on Jude, for goodness sake you'll be late!' Vicky shouted up the stairs as she waited impatiently for Jude to get his things together. He was busy getting the last of his things ready for his trip.

When he finally got down the stairs, Michael was waiting at the bottom, to see his son off before he himself went to work. Jude would be gone for a few weeks, the journey was planned well to fit in with his exams, before he went off to university.

'Jude this is your first trip of many without us, you make sure you take care and make sure you call us.'

'Of course I will Dad. In fact I'll call you tonight when I get there, how does that sound? Jeez, you worry too much.'

'Well it's your first trip without us, I know how important this trip is and I know what it means to you. Just stay safe okay?'

They both exchanged hugs before Michael left for work. Shortly followed by Vicky leaving the driveway in her own vehicle to take Jude to the airport.

The journey to the airport wasn't long. Pulling into the drop-off area, Vicky got out of the car and opened the trunk to get Jude's case out.

'You know Jude, I'm really proud of you for doing this. I've been so busy over the last few years and you helping me, supporting us all is... well I'm just so proud of you, thank you. Let me know when you get there, I've arranged for Max to meet you when you land and he'll take you to the hotel.'

'Thanks Mum, don't worry, I'll call you tonight when I get there.'

It was the first time Jude had flown on his own, but regardless of that, he was a mature and sensible young man. Now nineteen he wasn't just into girls and going out, his life was quite full with school and helping Vicky with her work. So jumping on a plane and taking a fairly short and routine flight was something he was looking forward to doing. He felt quite mature and grown up, handing his passport over and walking through airport security. When he arrived on the plane he had no problem in finding his seat and getting himself sorted for the short flight.

He placed his hand luggage in the upper compartment, some reading material in the seat pocket in front of him and buckled his seatbelt, ready for takeoff.

The flight wouldn't be long and he decided to get up to date with his itinerary for the coming few weeks. It was going to be a busy trip, but it would be the first of many and it was necessary for him to make the right impression with these people.

On landing, Jude had managed to get off the plane quickly, hoping he would escape the queue's of people with families going through security. However his fast transit off the plane was useless and he now stood with hundreds of other people waiting for the slow security staff to move into second gear. One by one the queue moved, snaking around the huge open room. Counting the number of rows and the number of people roughly in one of the rows, he assumed he would be in the queue for at least the next thirty minutes, possibly longer. So he pushed his EarPods into his ears and turned on some music.

It took forty five minutes to be seen and when he reached the security staff, they showed no sign of personality or desire to allow him to easily move on. Asking him questions of where he was staying, why he was here and who he'd be seeing. Their English was good, however Jude guessed their English was geared to just asking the same questions over and over again and not understanding the answers. So he kept his answers short and to the point. Even when he told them why he was there, they never once battered an eyelid or made any comment. It was clear they had no idea what he was talking about, either that of the fact they had little if not, no interest.

The immigration officer looked at Jude's photo a few times to the point that Jude even questioned himself that he was indeed the person in the passport. But eventually they let him go and he walked off to collect his luggage.

Moving through the airport, Jude was looking out for Max, who he was told would be standing near the exit with Jude's name on a board. Jude had met Max only once before, a few years back when he was in London at a conference with his mother. He'd been invited round for dinner, however Jude didn't remember what he looked like and was feeling anxious about missing him and being stranded at the airport alone.

From behind him, Jude heard his name called and he turned around, expecting to see Max with his name board aloft.

'Jude, over here!' Damian called, getting his attention by frantically waving his arms.

'Damian, my God, I had no idea you would be here, thank you. Have you come here to collect me? Mum told me Max was picking me up.'

'I told Maximiliano to allow me to pick you up, I got my licence last week, so I drove here.'

'What, you drove here on your own?' Jude asked.

'No, I'm not that brave, my sister came with me.'

'Who, Constantine, where is she?' Jude questioned, looking around.

'No, Sabrina's here. Look, she's over there.' Damian said whilst pointing over towards a seated area. Sabrina was busy looking after two young children and hadn't noticed Damian had already found Jude.

'Oh God I haven't seen her in years, are those her children? I've not met them yet. They were in Egypt with Asim when I met your sister last.'

'Come, let's go over there, I'll introduce you to my niece and nephew. Sabrina's looking forward to seeing you, you always make her laugh.'

It had been a few years since Jude saw Sabrina and a year since he'd last seen Damian in person. Over the years they all kept in contact and saw one another regularly. Vicky had ensured that Jude and Belle kept Damian in their lives as well as his sister and her husband Asim. Although an extended part of the family, they all caught up a few times a year and on the odd occasion met in person.

Jude regularly chatted with Damian on social media or on a video call at least a few times a month. They'd become very close friends over the years, regardless of the distance between them. Now they both had a common interest and that was one of the reasons why Jude had flown to Italy.

'It's going to be a busy few weeks Jude, there's not going to be much time for site seeing I'm afraid.'

'I know, I saw the itinerary you sent me the other day. Thanks by the way!'

'No problem, but I promise to take you around a few of the sites, now let's get you off to the hotel. By the way, I'm so sorry you can't stay with us whilst you're here, it's a really busy house with my sisters and brothers, aunt and uncle. They'd love to have you stay with us, in fact Serena wanted you to stay, but I insisted you actually liked staying in hotels and that you'd prefer it. I think you'll have to apologise when you see her, I think you've inadvertently hurt her feelings.' Damian said whilst looking away from the road and smiling at Jude.

'Don't worry about me Damian, just worry about the road. These Italian drivers are bad at the best of times, they don't need you driving into them like bumper cars.' When am I seeing your aunt and uncle by the way?'

'That's where we're going after we drop your bags at the hotel Jude. There's no rest for you I'm afraid, they're doing you dinner… and yes it will be a late one, we've a lot to discuss and celebrate.'

Jude spent the entire night being looked after by Serena. She'd not only looked after Damian like he was her own son, she had also looked after Jude or Vicky when either of them were in Italy. Vicky was in the city a few times a year and always made a point of seeing them all. She, like Serena, regarded Damian like her own son, always sending him cards, gifts, or money when he needed a little extra. It was her way of playing her part in his life, regardless of him not having lived with them in England. She had never been bitter over the fact they'd made the decision for Damian to live in Italy. She was content with the fact he needed his immediate family, though she had found it difficult initially leaving him. The two of them had grown quite close during the six weeks she'd been in Italy hunting his aunt and uncle. But on leaving Damian, she never went any more than a few days before contacting him. It was difficult to start with and Serena always had to be there to interpretative for them both. However over the years, Damian's English greatly improved and their conversations were regular and lengthy. She'd personally made a point of keeping in touch with Serena and always brought her gifts when she came to Rome.

Jude was an honoured guest in Serena's home and after being given more food than he'd ever eaten in one sitting, he'd asked if he could leave for the hotel. He was tired from the flight and long transit and wanted to get a good nights sleep to feel fresh for the morning. Tomorrow was going to be a big day.

Damian dropped Jude off at his hotel, pulling up right outside the entrance.

'There you go brother.' He said as he pulled the hand break up in his car.'

'Thanks again for a lovely night Damian, I'll meet you outside the main entrance to the office in the morning, eight AM right?'

Damian agreed and wished Jude a pleasant nights sleep.

Jude went into the hotel and straight up to his room. He got his clothes ready for the next day, washed and got into bed. After turning on the tele and finally relaxing, it didn't take him long to fall asleep. He always fell asleep with the tele on.

Jude's alarm went off at seven AM and he quickly jumped into the shower, then speedily got ready. He loved hotel breakfasts and shot down stairs to the restaurant, which gave him plenty of time to enjoy his food before a long day. The room was large with tables everywhere. It was quiet in the restaurant and after Jude had given the maitre d' his room number and name, he was given the choice of sitting anywhere he wished. So he opted for the balcony which over looked the street below. Sitting alone would have been too quiet and boring, but sitting, over-looking the people rushing by on their way to work, gave him some form of enjoyment.

Jude enjoyed every part of his breakfast and after, he made his way back to the room to wash up before heading out to meet Damian who was meeting him outside the office. Jude stopped at a coffee shop on the way to the office and picked up a cappuccino for himself and Damian. Walking out of the shop he could see Damian waiting outside the office for him. Jude ran across the road and briskly walked up the steps to where Damian was waiting.

'Good morning Damian.' Jude said, whilst handing him his coffee.

'Thanks, are you ready?'

'Yes, it's been a long time coming Damian, but this is what it's all about. What you do here today will be the start of things to come. People have to know your story and the stories of thousands of people who try to make the crossings each year. Oh and by the way you look good in a suit!'

'Thanks Jude, you too. I really appreciate you being here to support me. Your mum's here most of the year helping the cause. Allowing you to sit with me on this meeting means a lot. You didn't have to come though, but I'm grateful you're here.'

'No problem Damian, to be honest it's good to get over here for a change and see you, rather than you always making the trip to us. Plus I'm getting more involved all the time from home, so it's about time I started supporting you here in Italy.'

'Well the support is great and I know, that what we've got to push forward to the Cabinet will be enough to make some clear headway. After all, this isn't just about Italy, it's about every individual European country and one huge continent.'

'Come on.' Jude said. 'Lets get in there and start things off.

After leaving Damian with his aunt and uncle and returning to the UK, Vicky felt like she had to do something. Just staying at home and looking after the children was never going to be enough for her anymore. After a few weeks of being at home and getting back into the normal routine, she'd finally cracked it, she had an idea of what she wanted to do. But first she walked into the nearest local swimming pool and took out a full membership. If she was going to go all in, she was going to need a place where she could unwind and do something physical to get her mind away from things. She wasn't about to get back on a diving board, those days were long gone. But to get back in the pool and swim for fitness was something she was ready to do again.

That night Vicky picked up the phone and called Damian's aunt Serena. Vicky explained what she wanted to do and at some point soon, it would involve Damian and his story, with the additional help of his sister Sabrina. Whilst Vicky's heroics were still a viral hit online, she wanted to take advantage and start the ball rolling with regards to awareness of the dangers of illegal immigration across the Mediterranean. There was an underlining reason causing people to make the crossing and she would do what she could to make people aware of the dangers. That would be the first stage in what she hoped would be a journey she would take to stop people from crossing entirely. Firstly though, it would involve starting a donations page for her newly created charity. Shortly followed by Damian and Sabrina's story, how the decision was made to leave their town and make the long journey to Egypt. From there, the more difficult story would follow of what happened once they got to Egypt and when Damian got on the water with his mother and father. It was a story that people needed to know. It might just be enough to make a change… or at least be the first of many small steps to solve a problem that was getting worse each year. And at present, one which many Europeans simply couldn't comprehend, choosing to turn an eye to the expanding problem.

Sabrina and her two children were waiting on the steps of the office block where Damian and Jude had been all day. She knew roughly what time they'd be coming out and she wanted to be there when they did. Damian had made it clear on his various social media accounts what he was doing today but never once asked for support. Vicky had also added details of the meeting on her charity page and was getting much support from people all over the world. But like Damian, she had no idea that people were readying themselves to support Damian in a way they'd not done so before.

As Sabrina stood on the steps, she heard a few loud voices from around the corner. The voices gradually grew louder, then Sabrina heard a loud whistle. Somewhat startled, she told the children to stay where they were at the top of the steps, she ran to the bottom and looked around the corner. There was a group of people walking towards her with banners promoting Damian's cause. What initially looked like around twenty people walking towards the office was quickly increasing. The number of people making their way through the streets and around the corner never stopped and before she knew it, there were over three hundred people standing in front of the building. Each holding banners, whistling and shouting in support of Damian's cause. Sabrina had already ran back up to the top of the steps to explain to her children why the people were there and that they were helping their uncle Damian. The group of demonstrators weren't being violent or boisterous, they were doing exactly what they set out to do. To peacefully demonstrate and offer support to her brother. Sabrina stood at the top, staring down at the crowd. She felt so proud of both her brother and Vicky for starting all of this. Sabrina couldn't help but think back over the entire journey they'd taken. From the moment she saw Asim walking back to their home alone and without his friend, the militia taking over their village, to the long distance covered by foot before arriving in Egypt. The journey had been long and dangerous and their parents had lost their lives for its cause. Their story was told to the world and the book had become the best selling of that year. It had given Vicky's charity the kick start it needed and given her what she needed to take the first of what would be many steps to completing her own journey.

Damian and Jude had finished for the day. They'd consumed more coffee than at any other time in their lives, however it had been worth it. They'd made their points known and had heard from other nations, explaining what they would be doing. Vicky had joined them, video calling direct from the UK office, then allowing Damian to finish off the presentation. It had gone as planned and after, everyone from the meeting had shaken Damian's hand. Each delegate would play their part by supporting him and making him aware they would be committing both funding and personnel later in the year.

Damian and Jude walked out of the building, completely unaware of the demonstrators outside. Damian was first into the reception area and he could see through the two revolving doors there was something going on outside, some sort of commotion.

Pushing the doors around, he made his way outside and stood in front of the demonstration, in awe of its magnitude. As the entire crowd in front of him started to cheer and clap, more people joined in and the noise quickly became overwhelming. It had been a compete surprise to him, he had absolutely no idea there would be anyone here. He felt so proud of his work and it was clear from this crowd, that people were hearing his story and supporting their cause.

Sabrina turned to her brother and hugged him. They still had much work to do and their journey was far from over. Having the support from some major European countries was one thing, but now having the support from the people was recognition… their parents hadn't died for nothing.

Printed in Great Britain
by Amazon